Angel's House

Copyright © 1995 Alissa Whitehornne

Angel's House is a self-published novel.

First Printing: November 1995.
Second Printing: December 1995.

ISBN#:0-9649482-0-6

All Rights Reserved under international **Copyright Law.** Contents and/or cover may not be reproduced in whole or in part, in any form, (except for brief passages for review and promotional purposes) without the express written consent of the writer.

For more information, please write:

>Angel's House
>P.O. Box 6601
>Chesterfield, MO 63006-6601

Angel's House was printed by: IPC Graphics, Manchester, Missouri.

Cover design by: Gerard Atienza.

All products mentioned in this novel are trademarks of their respective companies.

Dedication

I dedicate this, my first novel, to the following beings:

God, for blessing me with my own special gifts, and equally as important, the courage to share them;

my husband who is my friend and most devoted fan, for loving me, believing in me and supporting my dreams;

my daughter who is the impetus of my writing this in the first place, because when she was born it became very clear that I had to be a woman who did not just talk about doing, but who actually did;

and my mother to whom I am eternally grateful for bringing me into this world, raising me well and always loving me unconditionally.

Special Thanks

I am also very thankful to my dearest friend, Kim L., who has always been there for me, and has always been a true friend, always.

In addition, I am thankful to three women whom I do not know personally, but who have nevertheless served as my personal role-models. They are beautiful, confident, positive and persistent. They are Oprah Winfrey, Susan L. Taylor, editor-in-chief of Essence magazine, and Author Bebe Moore Campbell.

To them, and all those previously mentioned, I say thank you from the bottom of my heart.

Acknowledgements

I have several people and organizations that I would be remiss if I were not to acknowledge them and their importance in my life.

First of all, Gerard Atienza, the artist who designed the cover of this novel for me. He is a young man I worked with for nearly two years at a company here in St. Louis. I believe he is an exceptionally talented artist, and I feel honored that he gave so much of his time and creative talent to bringing my dream to life.

During my senior year in high school, I was fortunate enough to have an English Literature teacher, Karen M., who had the courage to teach me how to write grammatically correct and with conviction.

I appreciate The St. Louis American newspaper, a Black weekly here, for giving me the opportunity to gain some much needed work experience after graduating from college.

I will always be grateful to the Urban League of Metropolitan St. Louis for giving me my first "real" job. It was there that I gained real confidence in myself as a professional.

I hope I will always remain good friends with a young woman, Marie B. She has always done whatever she could to help me network. Even when I had very little experience she believed in me. She could literally "see" my potential.

In addition, I have a network of friends, sorors and loving relatives who have always supported me.

I am very grateful to have had the opportunity to pursue my goal and to have gained so much support along the way.

I have been very blessed.

And Finally

To those of you reading this, I want you to know that this novel is my second baby, the first being my daughter. This second baby of mine may not be perfect but I did the very best I could to bring it to life, nourishing it with all the ideas, feelings, joys and pains, I've experienced and observed. And while it is fiction, I ask that you please read it kindly and gently, and without too critical an eye, because when you read it, you will be getting a glimpse into my heart and soul.

Enjoy.

*In loving memory
of my grandmother, A.H.,
(1903-1995)*

Chapter One

Angela and Baron Castlestone were living the life.

They entered the posh restaurant, Bradley's, smiling and dressed immaculately. She placed her black mink, which incidentally matched her jet black hair, in the safe hands of the hostess.

As violins played in the background, the waiters, dressed in starched, stark white, crisp shirts and perfectly pressed black uniforms, fell over themselves trying to wait on the Castlestones.

"Hello Mrs. Castlestone, what will you be having this evening?," the waiter asked.

"I'll have the shrimp carbonara, the house salad, white wine, Baron?"

"Yes, I'll have the filet mignon, medium well, your vegetable platter and the best red wine you have, not too dry."

Angela thought to herself. "Being Black when you are rich ain't so bad. Ain't so bad at all." Because she knew without her diamonds and mink, crisp speech, her handsome, well-groomed, impeccably dressed husband, she would be just another Black woman being told, "Oh sorry, we don't have any tables available." And being asked, "Would you like to see the sale rack?" Well, that wasn't a problem Angela Castlestone had.

Once the wine began to rush to her head, Angela got the nerve to ask Baron, "Well, do you think it's time?"

"Time?," Baron asked.

"Yes," Angela whispered, "to have a baby. I want our baby so bad."

"Soon baby, I promise. Just as soon as I get this promotion we will be set for life...," Baron tried to explain.

Angel's House

But the buzz Angela felt momentarily faded and the romance of the night was gone. Angela would have given up everything. Her new Mercedes, her minks, her diamonds, even all the incredible vacations she and Baron took, if only she could have a child.

Baron was everything Angela had hoped for in a man: successful, handsome, loving. He had even taken care of her every need. Except one. But he was so damned logical and sensible. Angela was 33 and the clock was ticking. She didn't want to be a scared-to-death 35 year-old running to the doctor every second worrying about everything, from miscarrying to Down's syndrome. Since everything else in her life was perfect, she also wanted the perfect pregnancy.

"Oh Baron, I can't wait much longer. Are you listening?," Angela asked sadly.

Baron hated this. He could feel tears welling up in his own eyes because he always wanted Angela to be happy.

"Excuse me." She rushed to the restroom to wipe away her tears.

Angela sat there in the plush surroundings of the ladies' restroom feeling embarrassed because she prided herself on maintaining control. She didn't want to ruin the evening. But why couldn't Baron just say yes, it was time? *She* knew it was time.

The restroom's female attendant approached Angela, "Are you okay?"

"Yes, I'm fine."

"You know, you don't see too many of us in this restaurant. You know what I mean? If you need anything, you just ask."

"Thank you," Angela said, now smiling.

Angela dried her tears. After all, it was only a matter of time. She had nothing to cry about. She had it all.

Baron looked up to see Angela returning to the table. She looked fine now, composed as usual.

But as he watched the now smiling Angela approach their table he kept asking himself if he had been wrong to make her wait so long.

****

That night when they returned home, Angela continued to smile even though inside she was still crying.

Before she got into bed she knelt on the floor on her side of the bed and prayed.

Angel's House

"Dear Lord, thank you so much for blessing me so abundantly. But Lord, could you please convince Baron that it's time?"

Ever since Angela could remember, this is how she prayed. On the night of her ninth birthday, she sat on the floor between her mother's legs while her mother oiled her scalp and braided her thick black hair into four large plats. Then Angela got into her white canopy bed and almost fell to sleep, exhausted from the day's festivities, when she remembered she'd almost forgotten to pray.

"Dear Lord, thank you so much for all the stuff I got for my birthday. I love my new bike and the clothes were really pretty. Thank you so much God for a great birthday. But God, could you please convince mother to let me get my ears pierced? Please God."

Two weeks later, Angela proudly wore gold stud earrings in her ears.

When she was 16 she prayed that Bobby Johnson, her high school's star quarterback, would notice her and ask her out.

Within a month, he asked her, "Will you be my lady?"

That night, she whispered, "Thank you God."

Alissa Whitehornne

And when she was in college, she prayed that she would meet her future husband. By her senior year, she had fallen in love with Baron.

God had always answered Angela's prayers. He was always there for her. Her mother had taught her to be prayerful and to believe in the Almighty God. Her mother had also taught her to be patient. But Angela had been praying for more than a year now, that Baron would agree to have a child, and still God had not answered.

Her mind told her to stand her ground and fight Baron on this issue, make a stand. But she had never argued with Baron because she hated fighting, and up until now, God had done all her fighting for her.

Chapter two

Days later, Angela busied about the house preparing for her ladies luncheon. Once a month, she and a group of friends got together to dish, have fun, talk about politics, children, and of course, men.

She dressed casually in designer sportswear, a pair of black Ellen Tracy slacks, softly pleated and cuffed, a silk sweater, a black and red cardigan by Dana Buchman, and a pair of black leather flats by Paloma.

Angela had been blessed with beautiful and flawless caramel colored skin. Most days she didn't wear any foundation at all, maybe just a little powder. Her jet black, shoulder-length hair was full of large bouncy curls. She was very slim and shapely with a small waist, full breasts and long shapely legs. Dressed in black and red, her signature colors, Angela was as stunning as ever.

"Cally?," Angela called, "Did you remember to get those strawberries from Newberrys?"

"Oh yes m'am, how could I forget them. You want to see them?," Cally answered.

"Oh no, I was just checking."

Angela was a perfectionist. She prided herself on doing everything just right.

The phone rang and Angela answered, "Hello, Castlestone res..."

"Darling it's me, Baron. I got the assignment. Your husband is the Chief Neurosurgeon at New Washington Medical," Baron said proudly.

"Oh Baron I'm so happy for you, for us. I can't wait to see you tonight, we'll celebrate," Angela said sweetly.

"See you this evening darling. I love you," Baron responded.

Angela's friends would be arriving any minute. Should she tell them or just wait a few days? They'd ask her a million questions and she didn't want to monopolize the conversation.

"Mrs. Castlestone that's the door, do you want me to get it?" Cally asked.

"Oh no of course not, I'll get it."

"Marianne girl come on in, it's so good to see you. Have a seat. Would you like a glass of wine, tea?"

"Nothing Angela right now. Since I'm the first one here I might as well take advantage. What's going on with you? How's Baron? Are you guys pregnant yet? Oh and the house looks so beautiful. Girlfriend, you and Baron are living the life."

"Marianne you need to quit but thanks. Everything is fabulous, Baron's fabulous and no, I'm not pregnant because I haven't been trying. How many times do I have to tell you that? Anyway, I am really happy. And you know how much I love my Baron. And mother and daddy are doing great. What's going on with you though? Any new men in your life who are not married or just broken up with a crazy girlfriend, you know what I mean?"

They both laughed. Angela felt especially grateful to Marianne because she was the only unmarried friend she had been able to hold onto. Actually, they had held onto each other.

Marianne was about 5 foot 6 with a small waist, luscious hips and a small, perky bosom.

She had dark coffee bean brown skin, soft, full lips and large almond-shaped eyes. She wore her dark brown hair in a pretty, short hair cut that always commanded a compliment. Today she wore a red pant suit with a bone-colored blouse and bone-colored suede pumps.

"I did meet this fine brother last week, so we'll see," Marianne said as if she could care less.

The rest of Angela's friends came soon, all dressed to the nines, all with successful careers, successful husbands, or both.

As usual, Caroline had to needle Angela, "Angela, you have got to get yourself a job. It is so incredible to have your own money and..."

Angela interrupted, "How often do you and Marcus have sex?"

"Angela!," Caroline was shocked to hear this from Angela, little miss perfect.

"Answer the question," Angela urged.

"I don't know, once or twice a week," a little embarrassed, Caroline answered with a lie.

Angel's House

"Baron and I? Every night. Every night." Angela spread the words out slowly like creamy butter on a warm slice of toast. "E-ve-ry night."

Angela hated acting this way but over the years Caroline had become so mean-spirited. Back in the days, she and Caroline had gotten along so well. But somehow Caroline had changed. She was a petite, fair-skinned, almost ivory-colored beauty with curly brown hair that went just below her shoulders. When she was in her twenties people used to comment on how beautiful she was, but as her personality soured, so had her looks. So much of her outer beauty, as with most people, had an awful lot to do with inner beauty too.

Angela added, "Either Marcus is too tired or you are, am I right? The point is Caroline, I am very happy with the way things are in my life. And besides," Angela added, "Baron's money is my money too. I think that's pretty obvious."

"Okay, okay let's get off this subject. What do you ladies think of the Republicans? I know half of you, or at least your husbands, are already Republicans. But what do you really think of them? I mean they've taken over Congress and that one gray-haired fellow. He scares me to death," Madeline finished what would begin a whole lot of talk. She had a master's degree, a Ph.D., and she loved a good debate.

Angela looked at Madeline and began, "I don't know about you guys. But I think this whole Republican landslide thing is like a wakeup call. Ever since November 8th a bell's been ringing in my head, "Wake up!"

"It's like it's us and them. The haves versus the have nots, Blacks against Whites, upper-class Blacks versus poor Blacks. But, we're all Black, aren't we? I see these trifling, ignorant, tore-up folks and I am so embarrassed and sad. A lot of White folk, and many Black folk too, seem to me to be washing their hands of some bacteria or disease. Like they've done all they can and they're through. Talking about putting children in orphanages. I don't know, I need more time to think about this. So much of what the Republicans say makes sense but something just isn't right."

Leslie chimed in, "I'll tell you what's not right. For some little hoodlums to be carrying guns and killing each other for nothing. It's not right for these stupid little girls to keep having babies when they are unmarried, uneducated and unemployed. Sure, they just keep having children and we keep giving them welfare. I'm all for welfare reform, hell maybe they need to get rid of it all together. I saw a news story the other night about how some people sell their food stamps to buy drugs. Why should I feel sorry for people who are lazy and immoral? What has the world come too? I have washed my hands. I'm sorry. I am through worrying about all these sorry Black, White and other races of people waiting for a hand out. I say sink or swim."

"Amen," several friends agreed.

"But wait a minute," Angela responded, "many people on welfare really need it and they couldn't all be lazy. Many people on welfare work too. The problem is that they make minimum wages, have children to raise, and they have no husbands to help. Okay, now you're thinking it's not your fault they don't have husbands. They should have thought about that before they got pregnant. Right? Well some of them didn't. And what about those children? Look at all of us. We made it because we are smart, hard-working, beautiful Black women. We also made it because almost every one of us grew up in two-parent homes, went to good schools, had all the contacts in the world, were nurtured, and the list goes on. We were fortunate. We can't just turn our backs on those who are less fortunate, can we?"

Leslie answered, "It's not about turning our backs on those less fortunate. Its about forcing people to take ownership of their lives. It's about people making their own way and not making excuses. It's about time we stopped putting money into programs that entrap instead of uplift. Angela, it's just time for a change."

Caroline added, "It's also about time to eat! I'm starving!"

Cally called out, "Ladies, lunch is served."

The ladies came to the dining room and viewed a lovely buffet of fresh strawberries and vegetables, assorted finger sandwiches and miniature European desserts. Every color fell right in place.

"Cally Jones you outdid yourself today, this looks lovely," one friend commented.

"Thank you," Cally replied.

Cally was a short, pretty, brown-skinned woman with a round face and a plump, round figure.

She was the Castlestone's cook, chef, caterer. She meant the world to Angela. She loved the fact that Angela was such a perfectionist and the fact that she was Black made Cally especially proud. Angela and Baron paid her well and they never treated her like hired help, more like an aunt for whom they cared very much.

A few minutes before everyone left, Angela announced, "Ladies, I just wanted you all to know that Baron got a new assignment today. He is the new Chief Neurosurgeon at New Washington Medical."

Everyone was thrilled for Angela, except for maybe Caroline, who kept thinking, "We'll never catch up now, never."

****

Once all her friends left, Angela's mind immediately shifted to plans for the evening. She called her family,

Baron's family and some of his close friends to invite them to a small celebration.

When Baron arrived he was only a little surprised to see all the cars in their circle drive. From the day Baron first met Angela, she had made him feel special, always remembering his birthday, special anniversaries and his important accomplishments.

He walked in trying to act surprised.

"Congratulations darling," Angela said as she met Baron with a warm hug and kiss.

The small gathering of friends congratulated Baron with a toast, then dined on hors d'oeuvres as Baron spoke to each person about his new assignment. Angela watched Baron as he worked the room wearing a charcoal grey suit. His skin, the color of a freshly dipped caramel apple, was as flawless as Angela's. He was tall and very slender. Dressed, he almost appeared lanky. But Angela knew that underneath the clothes were long, lean muscles. Baron was not skinny or lanky, he was a long, muscular, extremely handsome man with a well-groomed mustache and perfect, white teeth that he showed often with a dashing smile.

When the celebration was over and everyone was gone, Baron thanked Angela as he held her in his arms. Once he got her upstairs he seduced her slowly. Peeling off her clothes, kissing her neck, touching every part of her body as if it were the first time.

Their lovemaking was both exciting and comforting, warm and hot.

Chapter Three

Since Baron's promotion, all Angela could think about was having a baby. She believed that she would be ovulating for the next three days, today being the first day.

Over breakfast, Angela looked across the table at Baron and smiled. He looked especially handsome today, dressed in a navy suit, crisp white shirt and a floral tie that she had given him just a few weeks ago. She said, "I can't wait for you to come home tonight. Oh honey, I just know it's not going to take us long to get pregnant."

Baron said, "I'm just glad you're happy. We're going to have a beautiful little baby."

"Oh Baron," Angela cooed as she kissed him softly on the neck.

She walked him to the door, dressed in cream satin pajamas and a matching robe. He held her tightly and whispered in her ear, "Tonight's going to be wonderful."

And he was off for the day.

Angela rushed to the mall to shop. At her favorite lingerie store, she bought a cocoa-colored silk gown, matching satin slippers, and her favorite bubble bath.

While she bathed in the warm fragrant water, she thought about all the times she wished she were pregnant and how she kept agreeing with Baron when he'd say they needed to wait a little longer. For years Baron's schedule was too hectic for a child, at least that's what he thought. When he was growing up, his daddy was always busy working. And so Baron had promised himself that he would achieve his career goals first so that he could enjoy his son or daughter. Most of the men he knew had basicly let their wives raise the children alone while they pursued their medical careers.

Over the years, Baron and Angela had travelled all over the world, pursuing exciting, cutting edge career opportunities for Baron. Every move they made escalated his medical career.

Angel's House

Some people thought she married Baron because he was a doctor. But that was not true. She married Baron because she loved him, period. The fact that he was sexy, especially kind to her, romantic, extremely handsome, and ambitious were simply perks on top of everything else. And to be truthful, Angela was attracted to powerful men, always had been. And Angela could have worked and bought herself anything she wanted, because she was very bright in her own right. But she knew there would be time for her to pursue a career, later. For now, she loved being his adoring wife and could not wait to be the mother of his children.

Angela loved being Baron's support, his anchor.

Finally, they had settled in their hometown where New Washington Medical was located, and waited for this appointment.

Angela had understood Baron's plans up until the last six months. But, her maternal urges had grown with a vengeance. Every time she saw a baby she wanted to cry. She kept her feelings hidden most of the time, but that evening in the restaurant was a breaking point.

All Angela could do was thank God for Baron's assignment. Maybe Baron had been right all along. If he could wait till he was nearly 40, why couldn't she wait till she was 33? Well, she had waited patiently, most of the time, and her dream of having a baby was finally coming true.

Angela sent Cally home early, dressed in her new

gown and just waited. Usually reserved, Angela was almost giddy. At 5:15 pm when the phone rang, she could hardly contain herself. "Hello," she answered the phone anxiously.

"Mrs. Castlestone?"

"Yes."

"This is Megan Foster. Uhm, uhm at the hospital."

"Yes, how can I help you?"

"Baron, uhm, Dr. Castlestone m'am, he had a heart attack just a few moments ago."

"What?"

"I'm so sorry Mrs. Castlestone. I'm so sorry. He's dead."

Chapter four

The next week passed so quickly, Angela was almost in a daze. She managed with the help of her mother and father, to make plans for Baron's wake, funeral and burial. She didn't cry. Always polite, she would occasionally flash a small smile to make everyone else think that she was okay. By Sunday, November 20th, she finished her last thank you notes and placed them on a table in the foyer to be mailed the next day.

She slowly walked upstairs to her and Baron's room and retired for what she hoped would be forever.

The next morning Cally went to Angela's room and asked, "What do you want for breakfast?"

"Nothing," Angela replied.

But Cally went downstairs and made pancakes, scrambled eggs, fried bacon and squeezed fresh orange juice. She put it next to Angela's bed and left.

A few hours later Angela's mother arrived. When Cally told her that Angela hadn't come down yet she rushed upstairs to find her daughter just lying there in the bed, not asleep, but not really awake either. A plate full of cold food and an empty glass sat next to her on the nightstand.

"Angela?" Margaret whispered to her daughter.

"Baby you didn't eat a thing. You have to eat," Margaret said.

"I'm not hungry," Angela replied as she slowly turned away from her mother.

She just wanted everyone to leave her alone. Maybe if she lay there long enough, God would come get her too. Then she and Baron could have their family in heaven. She closed her eyes and prayed silently, "Dear Lord, please take me, I cannot make it alone."

He whispered back, "You are not alone and you are not leaving this earth, not yet." But Angela didn't hear Him. She just lay their in the darkness, waiting.

Angel's House

Through the silence though, came her mother's loving voice, "Well Angela your daddy's practice sure is doing well. He hired a new lady just the other day to answer his phones. Remember how you always said that other lady was so down and depressing? Well you'll just love this new lady."

Margaret was a tall, slim, elegant-looking, dark brown-skinned woman who was always well-dressed head to toe. She was an attractive, fiercely proud, 57 year-old woman who loved her daughter more than anything in this world.

Margaret went on and on for hours talking about everything that was going on in her, her husband's, and her friends' lives. She didn't know what to do, she just knew that her daughter needed her.

"Angela, maybe I should stay the night with you," Margaret said later that afternoon.

"No mother," Angela answered. "Please don't, I just want to be alone, please."

"Okay," Margaret hesitated. "Do you want to go downstairs for a minute to see all the flowers and plants you've gotten? They're beautiful."

Flowers? They filled the house with a dozen soft scents. But Angela couldn't smell them, didn't give a damn about some flowers. Her heart ached and her senses were so dulled that even if she had seen the flowers she wouldn't have been able to smell them.

"No thank you mother. Good night," Angela answered.

Margaret left and Cally returned upstairs with dinner. She cut her chicken in small pieces and cooked the vegetables so that they would be very soft and easy to eat. She also brought her glasses of juice and water, and a small bowl of vanilla ice cream.

When Cally returned a couple hours later, she found a plate full of cold food, an empty glass, a glass of warm water and a bowl of melted ice cream. She quietly removed the dishes from her room and said, "Good night Angela, I'll see you in the morning. I'll put those thank you notes in the mail for you too, okay?"

Angela whispered a barely audible, "Okay."

The following day, the same routine occurred, except this time Margaret ran a warm bath of water for Angela and forced her to get up and bathe. She lathered soap on her daughter's frail body, then rinsed all the soap away. She made her put on a comfortable white cotton gown and warm socks.

The next day, following their same routine, Margaret held her daughter in her arms and rocked her to sleep, "Hush little baby don't say a word, momma's gonna buy you a mocking bird, and if that mockin' bird don't sing, momma's gonna buy you a diamond ring..."

Angela fell asleep in her mother's arms. "Good night my baby," Margaret whispered, then kissed her daughter's forehead and went home.

Angel's House

By the end of the week, Cally had stopped cooking so much. She would just bring Angela several glasses of juice and a bowl of soup, hoping that she would just eat something.

That Sunday, Angela told her mother to stay home a couple days, that she had already done enough.

Monday morning Angela woke up when Cally arrived and asked her to make some strawberry crepes and to bring her a big glass of ice-cold milk.

"Crepes? Oh Angela, yes I'll make you crepes!," Cally said. She was so happy, she almost danced down the stairs.

Angela was famished after not eating for more than a week. So, for the next week she ate everything Cally brought her. And even though her body was finally growing stronger, her heart, her soul and her mind seemed weaker than ever. She felt like someone had reached through her chest and taken a chunk of her heart away. She thought to herself, "What I need is a heart surgeon." She almost laughed at her thoughts despite herself.

When Margaret arrived on a Wednesday morning, she was pleased to see that Angela was eating again. She chatted and ate with her daughter all day.

Finally, Angela asked, "Mother, why hasn't daddy come by to see me?"

"Because he can't bear to see you this way. It would break his heart. Now I can't bear to see you this way either, but I also can't bear not to see you. Do you understand what I'm saying? Angela don't you know that I will never forget how it felt to carry you in my stomach for nine months and then finally to give birth to you, my only daughter. No matter what, you will always be my baby."

Angela's father was fair-skinned with sandy-brown hair and just a hint of freckles. He was ambitious, serious and very loving. He was a good man, and even though he was not particularly good-looking, his average looks, coupled with Margaret's beautiful face and features, produced a prettier daughter than they would have ever imagined.

Angela walked over to her window and opened the blinds for the first time in weeks. The bright light made her squint as it invaded the gloomy, dark room.

"Mother, thank you for caring for me, just for being there. I don't know when this pain will go away but I do know that somehow I must go on."

Later that evening, Angela took a long soothing bath on her own. When she came out, Margaret was still there. Angela got into bed and looking like a child, she said, "Mommy, would you please rock me to sleep, one last time."

Margaret wrapped her arms around her only daughter's slim shoulders and rocked her back and forth, humming, "Lullaby, and goodnight, go to sleep my little baby."

Angel's House

And it was finally then that the tears came.

But Margaret just kept rocking her back and forth, back and forth, as she hummed, "Lullaby and goodnight, go to sleep my little baby."

****

Friday, December 2, 1994

Dear Diary,

I haven't written in you for some time but now that Baron's gone I think I'll have to. I have never been so lonely or scared in my entire life. First, mother and daddy always took care of me, then Baron came along and took over where they left off. Baron may have been pig-headed but he was a wonderful man.

I know I must go on. But how?

How does someone pick up all the broken pieces and meld them back together again? How, after being with Baron for the past 11 years, do I go on?

I sit here in this gloomy room of mine, with only a few streams of light, and my face damp with tears, and ask how?

I keep praying and praying but I get no answers. The only thing I can guess is that you just have to fake it for a while. Pretend you're fine and strong. Pretend that God has already answered your prayers.

Angela

CHAPTER FIVE

For several days Angela cried and when she slept she dreamed of her and Baron together. She'd reach over to touch him but always found nothing but a pillow. Slowly though, the dreams came less frequently and peace began to take hold of her.

On a cold, sunny December morning, Angela went for a brisk walk. As the wind slapped her in the face she could feel herself waking up. She saw cars passing by and children playing, and to her surprise she saw Christmas decorations everywhere. She couldn't believe

Angel's House

that Thanksgiving had come and gone and that Christmas was almost upon her.

When she returned home she had a cup of coffee in the kitchen with Cally. She asked Cally to whip up a quick lunch and dinner for her and to go home early. She took both of Cally's hands in hers and looked into her eyes, "I will always remember that you helped nurse me back. Thank you Cally. Now you just hurry up here and go home.

Enjoy your family."

Once Cally was gone, Angela picked up the phone. "Marianne, this is Angela."

"Oh Angela, I missed you so much. I tried calling but they said you weren't up to talking," Marianne offered apologetically.

"I know," Angela replied. "But do you think you could come by today after you leave work to help me do something?"

"Of course. I'll be there about six. See you then."

Angela was so happy to see her buddy. They embraced for a moment, then Angela put Marianne to work. "Marianne, I need your help. I want to move out of my and Baron's bedroom, but I can't go through the closets just yet. I just can't. I need you to move some of my things into one of the guest bedrooms. I'm going to sleep there for a while."

And so, Marianne went to work. About one and a half hours later she emerged victorious. "It's all set. If you need anything else let me know. No, I'll be back in a few days to see what else you need, okay?"

"It's a deal. Thanks Marianne."

Marianne held Angela closely and whispered in her ear, "You're going to be okay, I promise."

****

Exactly one week before Christmas, Angela was watching television late at night. On one of the cable channels she saw a handsome young minister preaching to a very small congregation. She was surprised because cable time was usually reserved for the larger churches.

The young minister said, "I guess you've all heard about the Republican's Contract with America. Well they might change the world, but I doubt it. You want to know what's going to make a difference? You. And you. You need to sign contract with yourself to make a difference in this world. Better yet, you need to sign a contract with God. Like the Republicans owe us a better America, we owe God better from ourselves. Everyone's so busy. They don't have time to deal with the problems going on in this city. You think the Republicans are going to make everything better? That they're going to clean up our streets and bring jobs to our cities. You think everything's going to be alright and we can just sit back and wait. Well as the young people say, 'You better ask somebody!'"

His confidence and uplifting sermon touched her. This was the kind of church to which Angela wanted to belong.

She couldn't bear the thought of returning to the church she and Baron belonged. First and foremost because she knew it would only remind her of Baron. And secondly, even though the people were nice, they lacked the kind of passion she needed in a church family. Sundays there were more like professional meetings, everything so matter-of-fact and unemotional. She wanted the choir to sing spirituals that made you weep but instead they kept a distance sounding more operatic than gospel.

Yes, she liked this young minister and his small congregation. She would visit them Christmas morning.

For that week Angela decided to put her worries behind her and focus on the upcoming Christmas weekend. She would shop for her nieces and nephews and her friends' kids. Immersing herself in the frivolity of the holidays would be much easier than dealing with the large hole in her heart.

On Christmas morning Angela dressed to go to City Church alone. She became a little frightened the closer she got because it was located on the rougher side of town. She almost turned around to go to her old church or even her parents' church, but something told her she would be okay.

She noticed people watching her as she approached the church doors. Upon entering she felt the church's warmth envelope her and she felt at home. She sat as close to the front as she could and waited. The singing was beautiful and the minister as handsome and eloquent as she remembered.

The choir clapped in unison as they swayed back and forth. Just as one voice faded away another equally moving voice would take over. They sang about "amazing grace" and faith that could move mountains. One song that particularly moved her was led by a heavy-set man with red hair, he sang, "Everything must change, nothing stays the same... Winter turns to spring... the young become the old..." Memories of Baron came rushing to her mind.

Next, the minister, in a commanding, upbeat, intelligent manner, spoke about the power of God, faith and prayer, how important it was that everyone believe.

The sun gleamed through the stained glass. She felt as if God were sitting next to her, wrapping his loving arms around her.

Suddenly though, Angela heard the church doors swing open and a wild-eyed, crazy-looking man burst into the church cursing and yelling, and brandishing a gun. His ratty brown clothes, which smelled of urine, hung on his thin frame. His eyes were bloodshot. He reeked of liquor. And his matted, dirty brown hair appeared to have not been combed in weeks.

Calmly the minister said, "Oh, you are not welcome here."

The wild-eyed man, shocked, said, "What? Listen mother..."

Angela thought she saw something fierce and strong loom behind the minister and a voice boom, "Get out!"

The man replied, "Okay." He ran out as fast as he could, leaving the gun behind.

The young minister smiled at Angela, a reassuring smile, because he knew how frightened she was.

Then he continued, "Brothers and sisters where there is faith, there is no fear."

Angela could not believe how calm everyone was. Were they crazy? Didn't they know that they could have all been killed? Her heart raced. She wanted to get up and leave but she was too frightened. What if he was still out there?

At the end of the service, Reverend Johnson approached Angela. "Welcome to our church sister. I'm the Reverend C.J. Johnson, and you are?"

"Hello, my name is Angela Castlestone. I saw you on television one night and you moved me," Angela said.

"Angela, I hope you don't think what happened today happens every Sunday because it doesn't."

Angela began to shake. Maybe these people were used to people on crack and people with guns. She began to get angry for putting herself in such jeopardy.

"The Lord sent you here for a reason. You know that don't you?," he asked.

"Well I uh. I," Angela didn't know what to say. "To get killed?"

"No, no Angela. Think about what you saw here today. You saw people with unquestionable faith push a madman out of our church."

"But I thought I saw...Wasn't there something behind you?"

****

Monday, December 26, 1994

Dear Diary,

I'm back.

Yesterday I went to a new church on the other side of town. I'm not sure if I was led to this church for a reason or not. But I could have sworn that I saw something behind that minister, something that would be menacing to someone evil, because the thing I saw didn't frighten me. Could it really be like the minister said, that those people's prayers manifested themselves into a creature that could frighten someone away? How could that be possible? Am I losing my mind? Maybe I saw nothing at all.

Angel's House

I keep asking God for answers. Right now the only message that seems to be coming to me is that that church and that neighborhood need me. Maybe it sounds arrogant for me to be so bold. But at this point, I have nothing to lose.

The tiny church looks like it needs so much, and even though its members were well-dressed and polite, outside the church was another matter. Just blocks away small children playing outside of run-down homes, broken glass everywhere. Beer bottles, 40 ounces, strewn along the neighborhood as if they were decorations. As I drove through this neighborhood, I searched for parents looking out for these children and found only a couple of young women screaming at their children, things like, "Boy you better get over here, before I woop your ass!"

No one ever spoke to me this way. None of my friends speak to their children this way. I don't know how such a large gap came about.

But it seems to me there is no time for speculation. Only a little time left for action. I think maybe I am supposed to help some of these people with the help of City Church. If that is the case, I will do everthing I can to help them.

Could it be that I am supposed to help others now? That I've had all the good times I'm going to have and now it's time to pay my dues for being so blessed. Until God answers me, I guess I'll just do the best I can.

Angela

Chapter six

In January, Angela insisted that the ladies luncheon be held at her house. She needed something to look forward to and something to keep her busy.

This particular luncheon seemed to center around gossip for some reason. Most of them were a little down. There was something about the period between the holidays and spring that seemed to gnaw at most of them.

Angel's House

For Angela, though, something else was bothering her. Her heart still ached something fierce and the loneliness was unbearable, because no friend or relative could fill the moments Baron had filled. Sometimes when she was at her worst she wondered if she should have loved him less. Wondered if she should have pursued a career like Marianne. Wondered if she should have done things differently. Maybe then his death wouldn't have hurt so bad. Maybe then she could enjoy all the money Baron had left her.

"Ladies," Angela began, "I have a proposition for you. I've been thinking, we've been meeting for a while now and it's been so much fun. In my loneliness, though, I've begun to question the meaning of my life."

"Now Angela...," one friend began trying to comfort her.

"No please, let me finish. This is not as complicated as I may be making it sound. I'm just wondering if there is more we can do to help others. I'm not preaching or putting anyone down, it's just a question. I just wonder if as a group we can put a dent in some of the problems that ail our city, particularly the inner city. Now I know some of you aren't as concerned about the Republican takeover as I am. But what harm could come from us trying to make a difference now? Why wait a few years and see what happens? By then it could be too late. Poor families could be poorer, a good school system for poor children could be non-existent, sex education could be stamped out all together, and affirmative action could be a distant memory."

The room fell silent for a moment.

They suggested a few ideas. Several of them defended themselves, citing all the examples of charity they had demonstrated. Eventually the conversation drifted back to idle conversation and gossip.

Today, Cally had served homemade black bean soup with gourmet tortilla chips, crisp vegetables and fresh fruit. As each person left, they thanked Cally for a delicious meal and hugged Angela warmly. A couple of friends, however, seemed to look at her with pity as if they thought she were losing her mind.

Marianne and Caroline stayed behind. They both understood what Angela was trying to say. Because even though neither had recently lost a loved one, they both felt an emptiness. The three of them made a pact that whenever they met for their luncheon, they would meet immediately afterward to discuss how they could make a difference in their city.

CHAPTER SEVEN

At the February meeting, the ladies luncheon was held at an expensive Italian restaurant downtown. Angela, Caroline and Marianne couldn't wait to talk.

When the rest of the group left, Marianne began, "I know what I want to do. I want to take in a foster child. I really do. I've already started the paperwork. So many Black children end up with White families and that's fine, but why not with someone like me. I mean let's face it, this may be the only way I'm going to have my own family."

Angela and Caroline thought her idea was great even though they disagreed with her comment about it being the only way she'd have a family.

"Marianne that's sounds great. Will your company accommodate your needs?," Angela asked.

"They'll have to," Marianne replied. "This is important to me and between my fax machine, business line, modem, voice mail, E-mail, all in my office at home, I know I can get the work done. They'll just *have* to accommodate me."

Marianne was the Vice President of Marketing for a company that developed and distributed competitive computer software. Her company did extensive research to see which software products were selling the best, then they developed similar products and sold them for less. As the Vice President of Marketing, Marianne managed two market research analysts, a public relations manager and a trade show manager. She also had an assistant. Even though Marianne loved her job, she needed more.

Marianne went on to explain that she thought it was time for her to take her happiness in her own hands. "You know I'd probably have a man by now if I weren't so smart and strong-willed. I mean sometimes I think brothers just assume I'm too tough or even mean. No offense Caroline, you're way meaner than me but it doesn't matter because you have those hazel eyes and..."

"What are you trying to say?," Caroline asked.

Angel's House

"I'm too dark for the kind of brother I want," Marianne answered honestly.

Angela and Caroline stared at each other dumbfounded.

"Don't look like that girlfriends because you know what I'm talking about," she added.

Angela did not want to discuss this issue. In her opinion it was old, negative and divisive. Here it was 1995 and they were still talking about skin color.

She also hated that she really did understand what Marianne was talking about. A year ago, she and Baron had gone to a dinner. It was an Alumni event for Black graduates of the prestigious university Baron had attended. At one point, Angela had scanned the room and realized that almost every one of those successful Black men of every hue, had married light-skinned Black women; in fact, her caramel-colored skin was on the dark side. It was almost like they belonged to some secret sorority. The pretty light-skinned girl sorority. She scanned the room once again, sure that she was wrong and realized that in the room of hundreds, she had only seen a hand-full of pretty brown-skinned women with men, and not one dark-skinned woman, they were all alone. It saddened her a little, made her feel a little guilty. It seemed that the light-skinned women were all tall, all slim and similar in demeanor, not one wore braids, not even a small afro.

Angela said, "Listen Marianne I know what you're talking about, okay? But can't we just move on? This issue has been discussed since slavery and it just won't go away. I am sick and tired of talking about it. Maybe that's easier for me to say because I'm a lighter shade of brown. But everyone has something to complain about, if they want to. Pretty blonde White ladies dye their hair brown so they will be treated with respect. Girls with short hair get weaves to feel prettier. I just think it would be better to cherish the gifts God gave us. Whether that means we're fat, short, tall, dark, light. I say treat whatever has been thrown our way as a gift. If you can change something safely, fine. But if you can't, why not embrace it?"

"Okay Miss Positive," Marianne smiled, "I know you're right and that's the way I feel most of the time. But sometimes you just have to vent. That's what I have you guys for."

Angela added, "That's what friends are for."

"You ladies are getting too mushy for me," Caroline interrupted. "Now let's talk about me," she continued, only half sarcastically. "I know what I want to do. I'm going to put my speaking skills to the test. Remember when we were in college how I was always speaking at some event? And I was pretty good. I already found one church that wants me to speak. I want to reach out to young women to tell them that they can be independent, strong and educated. Maybe I can convince a few of them that having babies is the wrong choice. I hope to get into some schools too and I'm going to put together some pamphlets."

They all agreed that Caroline's plan was ideal and would use her skills.

Angel's House

Then Angela confided to them that Baron had left her a substantial amount of money and that she wanted to put it to good use. She was a little frightened by the power the money gave her. She knew many women would have taken the money and ran. Gone on a cruise, shopped till the pain passed and lived comfortably for the rest of their lives. But she thought it was only fair that she share some of her wealth with those less fortunate. She told them about her experience at City Church. They listened to her story in shock.

Surprised, Caroline said, "Angela are you nuts going in that neighborhood?"

"Caroline I'll admit it's not the safest neighborhood," Marianne responded. "But don't forget that *that neighborhood* is filled with people like us who happen to be poor. Or maybe they're not poor but they prefer to live there. To tell you the truth I get treated better in those parts of town than in any other part. Just the other week I was getting some fried rice down there and..."

"Wait a minute you were *down there* getting fried rice?," Caroline asked.

"Yes. I know you sisters have convinced yourselves that the rice they serve in those fancy restaurants in your neighborhoods is just as good. But it's not. Sorry. As I was saying, I was getting some fried rice, shrimp fried rice, in case you were wondering, and the brothers down there think I am fine. I drive up in my BMW and when I get out of my car they are like, "Damn baby, you are fine!" Like it almost hurts them to look at me.

I have to be honest, it feels real good, for awhile anyway. Then I come back to the reality that they are younger than me, much less educated than me, are wearing jeans that are two sizes too big and I just know that the beeper they are wearing probably isn't there because they are a doctor or a businessman. Sometimes I wish I could take one home with me and teach him how to be what I need him to be: successful, career-minded, ambitious. It would probably be easier to teach an unsuccessful brother who already likes me to be successful, than it would be to teach one of those successful, fine brothers to like me."

"Marianne that's deep. I mean I just don't know what to say behind that," Angela said half jokingly and trying to get back to *her* story. "What I was trying to say is that this tiny church is perched in one of the poorest, most dangerous parts of the city and I think this minister can make a difference. But his church needs money to implement good programs. I want to do some research to see if that would be a good way to invest my money or not. I thought I'd talk to some business people and some of Baron's friends too to see if they'd want to pool their money, or at least their ideas. I'm not sure where this is going to take me. Right now you two have much more concrete plans than I have. But this is exciting. It feels good to know that our hearts are in the right places."

The three friends looked at each other and smiled. They knew that together their efforts would make a difference.

Chapter eight

At the March meeting, Marianne seemed somber. Naturally they urged Marianne to go first once the rest of the group left.

Marianne smiled a little and then began. "Well, like I told you guys, I wanted a foster child and that's just what I got. She was a pretty little brown girl with the saddest eyes I'd ever seen. She was only four years old. She was a crack baby and she ended up in the foster care system because her mother left her alone for two days.

I mean you guys tell me how a mother can do that."

Marianne tried to finish but she started crying.

Then she continued, "Well, she ended up with me. We both really liked each other. I put her in this great pre-school at my own expense. I bought her new clothes. And her poor little hair. Her mother had put all kinds of relaxers and crap in this little four year-old girl's hair. It was uneven and damaged. All around the edges was broken off. So I washed and conditioned her hair, oiled her scalp and braided her hair every night. You'd think no one had ever done that for her. I knew I wouldn't have her forever but I thought, I hoped, at least a month or two. After two weeks, her mother is ready to take her home. She supposedly went through some radical drug treatment program. After just two weeks, they took her away from me."

The three of them were silent for about a minute.

Marianne began again, "I know now that I need a child in my home. It wasn't the most painful experience I've had. It was the most wonderful. She was so perfect. I know I'm ready to adopt a child. I'm going to buy myself a house with a picket fence and adopt myself a little girl. And if that's going to be as good as it gets, that's good enough for me."

Angela and Caroline didn't even bother discussing how their month went, because compared to Marianne's, theirs was a cake walk.

****

Angel's House

Marianne went home later that evening and began writing in her journal.

March 17, 1995

What's up. It's me again. Do you think I fooled them? Do they believe that I am as sure as I sounded?

I can't forget about that little girl. No matter how hard I try. I see her pretty little face, hands outstretched, saying, "Mommy, please don't let them take me away."

But there was nothing I could do. Was there? I really did love having her in my home. I just know that if I move forward quickly, the loneliness will pass. I'm going to do everything within my power to adopt a little girl. I'm going to do everything within my power to adopt a little girl. I'm going to do everything I can...

Lonely and scared,
Marianne

Chapter nine

When April arrived, spring quietly descended upon this city and its surrounding suburbs.

Caroline was really beginning to feel good, better than she had in years. On this particular Saturday morning, she would be speaking to a group of young women who lived in one of the most notorious projects in the city. A group that held workshops and fairs throughout the city, had heard about Caroline and had asked her to speak at their springtime event.

Angel's House

Caroline wore a pale grey linen dress by one of her favorite designers, pale grey hose and pale grey, soft leather pumps. She wore her hair pulled back and styled in a conservative bun.

Even though she was a little apprehensive about driving alone to this neighborhood, she somehow had sensed that there was an angel watching over her. Since she, Angela and Marianne had begun this crusade of sorts, she had felt protected.

She spoke to about one hundred young women. As she stood in front of the podium on a makeshift stage, they eagerly awaited her words. She smiled and began, "I am here today because I care about all of you. I know that there is so much in each and every one of you that has yet to be discovered. Do you know how many awesome things that young Black women have accomplished over the years? Young Black women just like you who are smart and intelligent. Raise your hands if you know you are smart! Raise your hands if you know you can accomplish great things!" Only about half the girls raised their hands. And only about half of them meant it.

Caroline continued her speech, citing example after example of countless accomplishments by Black women.

She told them about Maya Angelou and how she progressed from being a scared girl who couldn't (wouldn't?) talk, to being an internationally known and respected author, poet and speaker.

About Madame C.J. Walker, America's first Black female millionaire.

About the courage of Harriet Tubman and how she navigated the underground railroad to free slaves.

About Carol Moseley-Braun, the first Black female senator.

And many others.

Their eyes seemed to narrow as they focussed on Caroline's face. The young women ranged in ages from 10 to 16.

"This is the only life you have. Live it well. Take charge of it. Because if you don't, someone else will. You don't have room in your lives for babies, not yet. And let me tell you, if you think you will follow in the footsteps of women who didn't work and lived off welfare, you will get your feelings hurt. The days of getting a handout are gone. You have the Republicans to thank for that. And I mean it, be thankful that you can't live off welfare. In some ways, welfare offers you a life with golden shackles, maybe worse than slavery because you don't even realize you are enslaved. If you have children too early, you will regret it for the rest of your lives. Raising children is the biggest responsibility anyone can take on, and without an education, a husband, and a good job, it is almost impossible."

Caroline walked away from the podium and set at the edge of the stage, urging her audience to move in closer. "I know that each and every one of you will achieve great things. Just live well and right. Work hard and study. Each night before you go to bed, look in the

Angel's House

mirror and tell yourself that you are an important part of this world. If there is no one else around who can share in your dreams, find someone who will."

Caroline ended her speech, "I thank you all for your time and attention."

As Caroline walked to her car, a teenage girl walked up to her. "Excuse me, excuse me," the young women called after Caroline.

Caroline turned around, "Yes, can I help you?" She stared at the girl's pretty, tan-colored cherub face which was filled with so much innocence, sadness, and despair. Dark brown, rope-like braids hung down her back and gigantic gold earrings hung from her ears. Her heavy tennis shoes looked like they were two sizes too big and her jeans did too. Her baby pink cotton-t-shirt was clean and neatly pressed and her lips were painted the brightest fuschia Caroline had ever seen.

The girl said, "I just want to know how you know that you're important. I mean how you really know you important? Ain't nobody ever told me I could do great things. My man, Dog, he standin' over there." She pointed to a young man dressed in baggy jeans and a white t-shirt. He had tiny little braids sprouting from his head. "He tell me I'm pretty all the time. But he still call me a 'ho' and a bitch. I tell him don't call me that, that I'm a lady. All I'm saying is how you know? Maybe it's because you grew up different from me."

Caroline looked at her, "I just know. Because we were all put on this earth for a reason. I just know."

The teenager interrupted, "Yo' man don't never call you no 'ho', does he? He probably treat you real good, don't he?"

Caroline replied, "No, my man doesn't call me a 'ho' and neither should yours."

The girl said, "Well I gotta go. Thank you for talkin' to me."

Caroline continued walking to her car but decided to turn around, "What's your name?," she called out to the girl. But she was gone. She looked across the lawn where the boyfriend had stood but he was gone too. It was as if the girl had vanished. But Caroline wanted to talk to her more. She wanted to tell her that her husband wasn't perfect. That even though he didn't call her a 'ho', he wasn't all that nice. She wanted to tell her that her husband was an arrogant, self-absorbed jerk that didn't seem to care all that much about her. But the girl was gone. She had asked Caroline a few questions and then she was gone.

Like a little angel she had disappeared into thin air.

As Caroline drove home, she couldn't get that girl's face out of her mind.

She also felt depressed as she recognized the difference between the area she had just left and the area she was returning to, her home. Where the projects were, she saw dozens of vacant buildings and graffiti everywhere. Just a few miles away, there were modest homes with neat lawns. And quite a few more miles

Angel's House

away, in the suburbs where Caroline lived, there were large homes with pillars, circle drives, swimming pools, children playing under the watchful eye of a parent, while the other parent was mowing the lawn, preparing lunch or telling the new gardener how they wanted the spring flowers to be arranged. They really did live in a different world. So many Black people had come so far. She wondered if people like her could ever really understand how it felt to be poor and ignored.

Caroline kept thinking about what the girl had said, "Yo' man don't never call you no 'ho', does he?"

Caroline's husband, Marcus, was a successful attorney vying for a coveted partnership with his firm. He was a tall, handsome man with smooth, dark-chocolate skin. His looks were model caliber. When they met in college it had been instant chemistry. Together, they made the kind of couple you see pictured in magazine ads. Together, they dreamed of a wonderful future, successful careers and of course, children. Caroline worked, shouldering the financial burden during those three years that Marcus attended law school. She'd cook him dinner every night, whatever he wanted. The apartment was always clean. And Caroline was always happy, smiling and supportive of Marcus.

Caroline thought that once Marcus finished law school and passed the bar their perfect life would begin. Marcus got a job with his first choice law firm but he didn't pass the bar exam the first time. If Caroline thought Marcus was intense before, now he was totally obsessed. He kept asking himself, "How could *he* have not passed the bar?" For six months he studied for his second shot, all along feeling humiliated. Most of the other new attorneys, all of whom were White, had passed the exam the first time. He passed the exam the second time with flying colors. Now, Caroline thought, our perfect life will begin. But Marcus kept saying he had to prove to those "White boys" that he was as good as them, then when he was *as good* he had to prove he was *better*. Being and staying the best was more than he bargained for. While he was fighting to stay above water, Caroline was drowning.

At first, Caroline tried to rekindle the romance that had been there in the beginning. In college they used to hold hands and go for long walks together. They would talk for hours about the things they would do to achieve their dreams. And the chemistry between them was like fire. The first time they kissed, she thought she'd explode, and so did he. The first time they made love, it was pure ecstasy for both of them. So, Caroline and Marcus could hardly believe that they had it all.

But being forgotten year after year had taken its toll on Caroline. They had hardly spoken at all for months and they rarely made love. Caroline filled the lonely moments with shopping. She could spend money faster than anyone she knew. She shopped when she was happy, which was rare; when she was sad, which was often; and when she was angry, which was almost always.

And so, as Caroline was returning to her large home in the suburbs, she began to wonder how long she could

Angel's House

tell young women how to live their lives when she wasn't living hers as she should.

When she returned home, Marcus was gone as usual. No note, no message, no nothing. Marcus was too busy to bother with little details.

Caroline simply got back into her car and went shopping. When she was shopping she was respected and in charge. She also felt loved. As she strolled into her favorite store, a small designer boutique, she was immediately greeted. "Hello, how are you today Mrs. Kelly? May I help you find something special?"

Caroline happily and boldly replied, "Of course, of course, I'm looking for something to wear to a dinner at the Ritz tonight. Any suggestions?"

"You bet. I'll be right back," the sales lady answered. She fussed about searching for something stunning and expensive.

Caroline always bought designer items and almost always paid full price because she prided herself on being the first to purchase this or that designer's new creation. It didn't even really matter if the dress was the right color for her complexion or if the cut positively accentuated her features. What mattered was that it was expensive and that everyone knew it.

Years before, what mattered to Caroline was that she was happy, healthy and pretty. She had always loved pretty clothes but she was never attracted to the most expensive, but to what most suited her taste, style and mood.

But Caroline was a long way from those days, and jeans, t-shirts and comfortable shoes were no longer a part of her wardrobe.

Once she selected the most expensive dress she could find in her size, she paid for it with her gold American Express Card.

Caroline's seven favorite words were, "Mrs. Kelly, how may I help you?"

****

Tonight, Caroline and Marcus were going to a charity dinner/dance to which his firm had bought several tables. She knew that he would not cancel on her since this event was work-related.

Later that evening, she slipped into her new dress looking rich and impressive but not really stunning or beautiful. As she leaned against the shiny marble counter, she waited and hoped for the hundredth time that Marcus would compliment her. "Oh you got a new dress," he said finally. And she held her breath for a moment thinking maybe he would say, "You look beautiful" or "I sure am a lucky man." But he said nothing else and instead focused on his handsome face in the mirror and his freshly pressed tuxedo.

That evening went like they always do. He socialized with everyone and she was bored to death. Marcus used to seem so proud of Caroline. He made her feel like a precious doll, too pretty to touch. But now he forgot her often. Only seldom referring to her as, "oh and this is my wife." Not "this is my sweetheart" like he used to or even "this is my lovely wife Caroline."

That night, after Marcus fell asleep, she got up, went downstairs to her sunroom, sat in a large wicker rocking chair and wept. She had been doing this for years and not once did Marcus wake up and notice. She often hoped he would wake up and ask her what was wrong. Wrap his arms around her and love her like he used to. Tell her everything was going to be okay.

This crying ritual that Caroline practiced almost every month began after she had two miscarriages.

The first time she got pregnant she let herself get so excited and happy. Even though things weren't going well between her and Marcus, she convinced herself that a child would make things better. Marcus seemed quite happy too. But just before she reached the twelfth week of her pregnancy she miscarried. The doctors weren't sure what went wrong. They just told her that nature had a way of getting rid of unhealthy things and that it was probably for the best.

The first few months were terrible, having to tell everyone that she lost her baby. She felt like a complete and utter failure. She couldn't get Marcus to notice her and now she couldn't even have a baby. To the rest of the world she was strong, bitter, but strong. At first, she tried to get Marcus to talk to her about it, but he was unavailable, emotionally. He kept telling her, "We'll just try again. Lots of people miscarry." But she wanted him to hold her. Tell her that he loved her and that everything would be fine. Tell her that it wasn't her fault. But he couldn't do that because he kept thinking it was his fault. He couldn't make Caroline happy, and now they couldn't even have a baby.

Living under the same roof, they might as well have been living in two different worlds.

It took Caroline nearly a year before she got the courage to try to get pregnant again. This time she told no one except for Marcus. When she made it to the twelfth week she thought she was home free. But one week later she miscarried again. This time Marcus was even more unavailable. It broke his heart to see Caroline so depressed but he didn't know how to comfort her.

Once again, they retreated into their own private worlds.

And now, here she was telling young women to take charge of their lives and that they could be happy. She realized that now on top of everything else, she was a fraud.

Sunday morning, Caroline prepared breakfast for Marcus. He was shocked because she hadn't cooked in months.

"Marcus, we need to talk. I haven't been happy for a long time. We need to work on our marriage," she said.

Angel's House

"Ahh Caroline, come on. I don't have time for this crap. I'm doing the best I can. You know I'm up for that partnership," Marcus said.

"But Marcus, don't I count? There's always something. Sooner or later, I have to come first."

"Damn Caroline, you think you don't come first? You shop all the damn time and I never complain. You have a beautiful, big ass house. I let you do whatever the hell you want to do with the money you make, and all you want to do is complain. Can a brother get a break here?"

"First of all we got this house so you could impress all your friends and all your co-workers. I never wanted this house. Secondly, I offered to pay some of the bills with my money but you had to be the big shot. 'Naw baby, you take your money and have fun, I'll take care of the important stuff.' This is not about the house or how much I shop, it's about us. Our marriage is falling apart. Why can't you be home more often? Why do you have to work all the time?"

"Because I want to make partner damn it! How many times do I have to say that! Once I make partner, everything's going to be better. You'll see," he said angrily.

"Sure Marcus, whatever you say," Caroline replied, defeated.

What she wanted to tell him was that she still loved him and that she needed him desperately, but that would have made her feel too vulnerable.

What he wanted to tell her was that he was scared that if he didn't put in all the hours he would fail. He wanted to tell her that he missed touching her, kissing her and loving her. He wanted to tell her that he missed her pretty smile.

Sometimes he wished he could put their lives in reverse and go back to the way things used to be. If he had been honest with her, he would have told her that he wasn't even sure he wanted to be a lawyer anymore. But he couldn't. He just couldn't. Because that would have made him feel like the biggest failure of all.

Marcus went to the office to prepare for an upcoming case and Caroline went to church alone.

When she returned home, she started browsing through the Sunday Classifieds. "House for rent. Two bedrooms. Furnished with antiques. Quaint. Wraparound porch. Great rent!"

Monday afternoon, Caroline went to see the house for rent. It was nestled in a quiet culdesac in a middle-class neighborhood on the outskirts of town. It was a two-story, Victorian-styled home painted slate blue with white trim. A white porch swing dangled in the spring breeze. Dozens of huge, old trees filled the neighborhood. She could see a pond in the backyard filled with ducks. She walked up the freshly painted white porch to meet the elderly White woman who owned the home.

"Hello, I'm Caroline. I'm here to see the house."

Angel's House

"I'm Alice Johnson. I've been expecting you. Please, come inside so I can show you my home." Alice was a petite White lady with super soft, slightly wrinkled skin that looked like it had never been touched by the sun. She wore a pair of navy slacks, white tennis shoes and a white t-shirt decorated with flowers. Her white hair was cut short and permed softly. It delicately framed her sweet face.

Alice showed her the two cozy bedrooms, a sunroom drenched by sunlight, the old-fashioned kitchen with a big refrigerator that must have been 50 years old. The wood floors were polished so that they shined, and beautiful, old rugs accented almost every room. The charm and warmth of the home was intoxicating.

"I'm going to be leaving this weekend to help my sister out in Oklahoma. She's got cancer and I don't know how much longer she's going to live. I don't want to leave my house empty. Maybe it's old-fashioned but I just think a house will fall apart if no one lives there. Do you like it?" Alice asked.

"Oh yes, I do," Caroline answered.

"Well, then why don't you come stay here? I'll be gone for several months. I've trusted my instincts all my life and I've never been wrong. I want you to stay here. I won't charge you much and I'll pay the utilities in advance. You come stay here for a while. I've lived here for fifty years and this home brought me and my husband many years of happiness. He's dead now but the memories are still alive. You bring all your own towels and linens. I'll put my things away so you can feel like this is your home. Why don't you come stay here for awhile?"

"I'm sorry, I need more time to make this decision. It's all so sudden. I'll let you know," Caroline said. But as she walked back to her car she could feel something invisible and gentle calling her back. The same little angel that had been protecting her wanted her to stay awhile too.

"I'll take it," Caroline told the lady.

The following week, Caroline prepared to leave Marcus. She purchased a few small items and filled her Louis Vuitton luggage with as many clothes as she could. Marcus didn't even notice what she was doing.

The following Saturday morning she left a note for Marcus that simply read, "I'm out. Caroline." In the back of her mind she could see Jade singing, "5-4-3-2. Your time is up!" She felt like dancing.

****

That afternoon, she moved into the blue and white Victorian home. She unpacked her clothes and neatly put them away. That evening, she made herself a sandwich and drank a glass of ice tea. On the kitchen table, she noticed several small booklets with pretty scenery on the front. She started reading them and discovered uplifting, positive messages about God, life and herself. She couldn't believe these little booklets could contain so much wisdom.

Angel's House

Caroline hadn't been raised in a particularly religious home. And even though she had found a church home last year, there was still something missing. She always felt like her fellow worshipers had a connection she didn't have, like they had a number that she couldn't find in any phone book, from any operator. She felt like she was desperately trying to find an unlisted phone number. So she just kept dialing and dialing and always got the wrong number.

When Caroline was 10 years old, her mother was always there to comfort her and give her advice. One day her mother asked her, "What's wrong sweetie?"

"Mommy, I feel sad."

"Why honey?"

"Because Kelly doesn't want to be my friend anymore. She says I think I'm cute."

"Don't pay her any attention. She's just jealous of you because you have good hair and light skin. I went through the same thing myself. Don't pay them any attention. You have to be thankful for being so pretty, it's a gift."

"From God mommy?"

"Yes darling, you thank God every day for your looks. Then use them to your best ability."

"I don't understand."

"Use them to get what you want. Don't worry about those other people. Having close female friends will always be hard. Use what you've got, to get what you want. You'll understand when you get older."

Over the years, Caroline observed how her mother "used" her looks. It seemed to work most of the time, but by the time she was a teenager, she noticed that her father didn't seem as interested in her mother as he used to be. From that point on, her mother often fell into a deep depression.

So, years later, sitting alone in this house, Caroline read little books that talked to her the way she wished her mother had. That night, before she went to bed, she prayed and made a connection for the first time in years, "Dear Lord, please show me the way."

****

Sunday morning Caroline was awakened by singing birds just outside her window. She smiled as she watched shadows dance across the yellow wallpaper decorated with white and pink roses. And then, in the back of her mind she felt a nagging feeling, like she had forgotten something. She sat there for a minute, puzzled. Then it hit her, she realized that her period was late.

She panicked, ran to her luggage to retrieve an old pregnancy test, and nervously administered it.

Caroline couldn't believe it. She was pregnant again.

Angel's House

****

Later on that day, Caroline found an old spiral notebook in Alice's kitchen and decided for the first time to keep a diary, a journal, whatever. She'd heard Angela and Marianne mention how this practice helped them.

It's Sunday, April 16, 1995. Oh my God it's Easter and I didn't even go to church today.

Well today I thought I'd start a little book, I guess I'll call you Caroline's little book.

Things aren't going so well for me lately. I've left my husband and I'm pregnant. I don't know which is worst. I really do still love Marcus. But he makes me feel like crap. Sometimes I feel like he's looking straight through me. It seems like he doesn't see me at all. Not me as his partner or friend, his lover or wife. I'm just a piece in a chess game, something to move around so that he can reach his goals. I always wanted Marcus to be successful, but why did the price have to be so high?

It didn't happen over night. I mean it's not like we were happy one day and the next day we were miserable.

It happened so slowly. One night he wouldn't be home for dinner because a meeting ran over and I said, "That's okay honey, I'll just freeze the leftovers."

Then one night a week turns into two, then three.

Soon he's not calling at all. Just assuming I'll understand because he's trying to reach a goal.

Then I thought getting a job would fill the emptiness I was feeling. And for a while it helps. But by then I'm miscarrying, losing my little babies. And there's no one to talk to, no one to understand. Each time I just knew I was going to have my babies. I took so much for granted. My looks, my marriage, my unborn babies.

I always thought my looks would be enough to get what I wanted. What a crock! I thought being married would be so easy. I loved him and he loved me. That should have been enough. But it wasn't. Sometimes it seems like love has nothing to do with anything at all. Maybe I never even knew the true meaning of love. Now I know that love does not grow on its own, that it needs a lot of help. Kind of like a garden. But you see I never had a garden and when we got our home we hired a gardener to do the work for us.

But no one can keep our marriage together but us. I don't know how we could have been so stupid to believe our marriage would survive without communication, honesty and respect. But no one told him or me. We were young and in love, and more naive than we knew.

And I don't know how, or if, I will ever get over my miscarriages. I've wanted a baby for so long now that it seems all I can feel is the pain and disappointment. I'm so scared to be hopeful, but I'm scared of being cynical too because what if the baby can sense my negativity. What if he or she knows how weary I am?

Angel's House

For now, I must focus on myself and my baby. If Marcus wants to be a part of our lives, he'll have to make the first move. Oh dear God, please, help this baby make it. I'd do almost anything...

Caroline

Chapter ten

Marianne was busy and happy. She couldn't wait to attend her first adoption meeting. Before the adoption agency would even consider her, she had to attend two seminars that prepared and warned prospective parents about the joys and challenges of being a parent.

Dressed in navy pumps, navy slacks and a crisp white linen blouse, Marianne carried her navy blazer on one arm as she anxiously walked into the agency's meeting room. Several anxious, professional-looking couples sat

Angel's House

with her, excited to get things started. Just before the meeting began, a large, teddy-bear, lumber-jack looking brother sat next to Marianne. The brown-skinned man had a neat mustache and beard. He wore jeans, a white t-shirt and white Nikes. His wavy hair was pulled back in a pony-tail. Marianne thought to herself, "Get real my brother. No suit, no tie? Are you serious?"

He looked over at her and said in a whisper, "Hello," not wanting to interrupt the speaker who had just arrived. He had gorgeous light brown eyes that made her uncomfortable. She said, "Hello," in return and quickly turned her attention to the speaker.

The speaker, a 40ish, small and slender Black man, tried his best to be honest about the responsibility of being an adoptive parent. He kept pushing his glasses back as they slid down the bridge of his nose.

"Now, it's not that we want to scare anyone off, its just that this is an extraordinary experience meant for extraordinary people. We can't afford to have a parent trying to bring a child back. The price the child pays in self-esteem is far too high. So, we want you to know that some of the children are near perfect and some aren't. Do any of you have questions? If not, we will now show the video."

Marianne was so excited she thought she'd burst. There was absolutely, positively nothing the man could say that would frighten her away.

After the video was over, refreshments were served.

The man sitting next to Marianne, went straight to the refreshments. She thought, well he is a big man. He returned with a plate of hors d'oeuvres. "Would you like me to get you something?," he asked.

"No thank you."

"My name's Joe Washington. What's yours?"

"Marianne. Marianne Jones."

"Well I tell you, I don't know if I'm up to the task. I don't think I'm ready. I thought I was, but now I'm not so sure," Joe said.

"Well I know I'm sure. I can't wait."

"Really?," he was surprised. "Being single makes adopting a little more complicated. I'm sorry, I just assumed you were single."

"I am."

"I'm divorced."

Marianne wanted to ask how many times but she thought that would be rude.

When Marianne saw an opportunity to talk with the agency's director, she excused herself, "Joe, it was nice meeting you."

"You too Marianne."

Angel's House

But when she returned, Joe was still there. He offered to walk her to her car. When she declined, he simply said good night and left.

****

At the second meeting, Marianne was surprised to see Joe there.

Dressed in a kelly green short-sleeved coatdress with gold buttons, Marianne sat down next to Joe. "I thought you said you weren't interested," she teased him a little.

"What would you say if I told you I came back to see you?," he said, teasing her too.

"Yeah right," Marianne said, blushing.

"I'm serious. Afterwards, lets go out for a drink. Okay?"

"I don't know. I'll think about it. Let's just see how the meeting goes." Marianne couldn't believe she said she'd think about it.

Today, Joe wore a purple warm-up suit with a bright white t-shirt underneath. Marianne noted that he looked squeaky clean, like he'd just stepped out of the shower. Well, clean or not, Joe was not her type. As far as she was concerned he was a 'round the way kind of brother. Even though he didn't have a gold tooth, or baggy jeans, she could tell. Plus, she was almost sure he had a curl and she hated curls.

Once the meeting was over, Joe asked Marianne if she was still sure she wanted to adopt.

"I'm positive."

Joe said, "With my business, I just don't know if I have time. I'm so busy."

Marianne thought, "I've heard this line before." "My business." He probably sells t-shirts at the baseball games. Or historic baseball caps when the Black Expo comes to town. But his real job was probably delivering the mail or driving a truck. Or maybe he was even a teacher. Either way, it didn't matter, because he wasn't her type.

Joe continued, "There's a restaurant across the street if you'd like to have a drink or a bite to eat. I can't go much further than that today. My Benz is in the shop and I'm cabbing it a few days."

Marianne thought, "Oh no! This is too typical." She fought back the urge to say, "And my Jag's in the shop, what a bummer."

He went on to say, "If the part doesn't come in soon, I guess I'll go ahead and get a rental."

She almost wanted to laugh right in his face, because she'd heard all the lines before. Here she was the Vice President of Marketing for a computer software company talking to this tired brother. But he really was cute and those light brown eyes, *ooh,* and those light brown eyes.

Angel's House

****

Marianne couldn't resist Joe's invitation. He held her arm as they crossed the dark street to reach the restaurant. Once seated in the restaurant, he kept staring at her. Finally she asked him, "Why are you staring at me, is there something on my face?"

"I'm sorry if I was rude, really. I just think that you are really a very, very pretty lady. But I shouldn't stare, that's rude. But, you do have really pretty eyes, you know."

"Me?," Marianne questioned. "Now Joe, you are the one with pretty eyes." She said it before she had time to think. She didn't want to lead him on.

"Thank you," Joe said, blushing. He thought to himself, "She does like me! I knew it."

"Joe, I don't want to lead you on, you seem like a very nice guy, but..."

He interrupted her, "Marianne why don't you tell me a little more about yourself, where you work, what you do, what makes you happy."

"Seriously?," Marianne asked, genuinely pleased. She hadn't met a man in years who really wanted to know more about her.

"Of course I'm serious", Joe said, a little annoyed for the first time. "I don't play games.

I don't have time to play games. You can count on two things: that I am for real and that I like you, seriously."

And with that, Marianne relaxed and began talking about herself. Joe listened attentively, only occasionally interjecting an, "oh really" or "that's interesting," but mostly he just listened.

By the time she stopped talking, two hours had past.

"Oh my goodness look at the time! I have to get out of here," Marianne said.

Then she sat back for a moment, realizing how good she felt. For the past two hours Joe never interrupted her to show off his business or technical acumen. So many other men would have dropped in a little computer lingo to let her know he was computer literate, maybe even talked about his hard drive crashing on his laptop when he was flying to New York on a business trip. So many men would have given her suggestions on how she could have increased sales with an alternative marketing strategy that they had implemented at their company. But not Joe. He just listened to Marianne talk.

Marianne leaned forward and put her hand on his stubbly cheek. She said, "Joe, you are so sweet." And for a moment she let herself imagine what if, what if she leaned over and kissed him, felt the tickle of his mustache on her face, tasted the sweetness of his tongue in her mouth and...

Angel's House

"Oh Joe, I really have to go," Marianne said.

"Of course, it is getting late. But first, let me get your phone number."

****

Marianne was feeling confused. Part of her wanted to just focus on adopting a child. And part of her wanted to let Joe into her world too. She felt like she had so little time to waste these days, like if she didn't grab hold of everything it would all slip away. Her biggest fear was to turn 40 and be alone, husbandless and childless. She hated the thought of looking back and realizing she had made big mistakes.

She gazed out the window, sitting in her large office decorated with antique cherry wood furniture and beautiful photographs framed in cherry wood. She wondered why what she had wasn't enough. Very few people her age had made it like she had. But at 34, she knew there was more to life than work. If someone had told her that this was it, that nothing else fulfilling and good was coming her way, she would have wanted to die. This was why she had to adopt a child now. Because in her mind, time was running out. She hoped that she was adopting for all the right reasons. She hoped she wasn't being selfish. Because that wouldn't have been fair to a child. As she thought it through, she convinced herself once again, that she was doing it for the right reasons, that she would be a great mother and that God would also guide the right man in her direction.

Soon she recognized that she was daydreaming, something she had little time to do. She took a deep breath and dug into the project at hand.

"Marianne," Karen interrupted her train of thought. "There's a Mr. Washington on the line, do you want to take the call?"

"Marianne?," Karen called her name again over the speaker phone. "Do you want to take the call?"

"Sorry Karen, yes, I'll take it. Hello Mr. Washington. How are you doing today."

"I'm just fine Ms. Jones. Are you having a busy day?"

"Yes I am, as usual."

"Will you be busy tonight?"

She hesitated.

"Come on Marianne you heard me. Would you like go out to dinner with me tonight?"

"Why don't you come over to my place. The weather's nice. We could barbecue out on my patio, listen to some music."

"That sounds great. How's seven sound?" Joe asked.

"That sounds good to me. Let me give you my address." She gave him directions with just a bit of smugness because her apartment was located in one of the hippest, most expensive areas.

"Oh that's a really nice area. What shall I bring?"

"Just yourself. Next time, you treat."

"See you then," he said.

"Good bye Joe."

Marianne could feel the ice melting away from her heart. There was something about Joe and it wasn't just those light brown eyes. He seemed so genuine and real. Even though she knew things probably wouldn't work out, she figured there was no harm in having a little fun with a really nice guy.

****

After work, Marianne stopped at the grocery store to pick up some steaks and chicken, some items to make a salad. On her way home, she wished she had gotten something sweet too, but she was running out of time.

When she got home, she took off her brown linen suit and cream-colored silk blouse, showered quickly, then dressed comfortably in a pair of brown silk, full-legged pants with a drawstring and an off-the-shoulder, body-hugging, brown, crushed silk blouse. She slid into a pair of low-heeled metallic mules and if she had realized just how pretty and sexy she looked, she would have changed into a pair of sweats because she didn't want to lead Joe on.

She added a few curls with a steaming hot curling iron and touched up her makeup. Just as she was walking into the living room to straighten up a bit, the doorbell rang. She felt her heart skip a beat.

"Hello Joe, come in."

"This is a beautiful place," Joe complimented.

"Thank you." Marianne wanted to ask him what his place was like but she didn't want to embarrass him. A simple thank you was enough for now.

Her apartment was decorated neatly and elegantly in cream, everywhere. Cream carpeting, cream walls, cream leather sofa and chairs. He wondered how she kept it so clean.

"Do you have a housekeeper?," Joe asked.

"Yes. But she only comes every couple weeks," Marianne said nonchalantly. The truth was that she came every week, always at 7 am, every Saturday. But she didn't want Joe to think she was a snob or that she thought she was too good to clean her own apartment.

"Well, this is beautiful."

"Thanks again. What would you like to drink?," Marianne asked.

"Why don't we open this bottle of wine," Joe recommended. In his hands he held a bottle of expensive wine and a box of candy.

Angel's House

"Okay." Marianne took the bottle and the chocolates into the kitchen.

Joe stood there for a moment, truly pleased. Marianne really has her stuff together, he thought. He had to remember not to stare at her too. Because tonight she looked so good he could hardly keep himself from getting turned on.

"Have you started the grill yet?" he asked.

"Not yet, it's a gas grill though so it won't take long," she said.

He wandered onto the patio to find a large gas grill that looked new and a small, old-fashioned barbecue grill, the kind that actually used coal and fuel. By the time Marianne reached him with his glass of wine, he had started up the fire on the small grill.

"Joe, you didn't have to do that. The gas grill works fine."

"I know but I like the way the old grills make food taste. Now really, don't you prefer that too?"

She had to admit that she agreed with him. That was probably why she couldn't bring herself to part with the older grill. But it was always so hard to use and it took her forever to get a fire started, and even longer to clean it. And she was always afraid something would happen and she'd burn down the entire building.

"Well the gas grill works fine," she mumbled as she

headed back to the kitchen, then she turned back around, "but thank you, that was a nice thing to do."

"No problem."

Marianne seasoned the meat, then Joe barbecued while she made the salad. Then she put on a couple CD's, Barry White and Marvin Gaye. They ate together in her dining room listening to the music. The sun was just going down and from the open patio door, a cool breeze entered the room silently. They walked into the living room which was just off the patio. She sat on the sofa and he in a chair just across from her. He could see her stomach because when she sat down because there was a small gap between the drawstring on her pants and her top. But Joe just played it cool.

"Are you getting too cool?" he asked.

"Actually, yes."

Joe rose and went to the sliding patio doors. "It sure is a beautiful night." He savored the night for a moment before closing out the cool night air.

Marianne watched him, dressed in Levi's, those leather work boots that so many of the teenagers wore these days, and a nice, neatly pressed navy and brown striped shirt. Upon closer inspection, Marianne began to doubt that he had a curl afterall. It looked like his hair was just naturally wavy. She was embarrassed for being so critical. She also noticed that even though he was a big man, he probably was not overweight. He actually had a small waist, large chest and arms, and an adorable, tight backside.

When Joe sat down, he sat next to her. "Dinner was great. Thank you for asking me over."

"Thank you for calling me today. This was really nice."

"Yeah it was." They gazed into each others eyes. He wanted to take off her blouse, those silk pants. He wanted her so bad he didn't know what to do. He wasn't sure, but he thought he saw the same longing in her eyes.

He broke the eye contact though and began talking about the news. A young girl had been killed at a local school. "It's just a shame, isn't it? That kids can't just be kids anymore. When I was in school things were so much safer."

Then they started talking about their high school days, the people they knew. It turned out that he was a few years older than her, and they also ran in different circles, but they still had fun talking about the good ol' days.

At one point, Marianne retrieved the chocolates from the kitchen. They were delicious. Joe finally got the nerve to lift one from the box to feed her. She almost licked the excess chocolate from his fingers, but resisted the temptation. They both fought to keep the evening light and friendly.

Talking to Joe was so easy and fun. Time flew by

and when it was time for him to go she wasn't tired, but energized. She walked him to the door. He put his arms around her slim waist and gently and quickly kissed her lips.

She slowly closed the door and rested her back gently against it for a few moments, then she thought, "what the hell" and swung open the door.

"Joe...," Marianne called out. But it was too late. He was gone.

****

The adoption process was going very well and Marianne thought about her future daughter all the time. She wondered who she would get, what she would be like, how they would get along. This was the most exciting thing to ever happen in Marianne's life. Not only was she helping a child, but she was also helping herself. She imagined that she and her daughter would shop together at the mall, have lunch, then go to a matinee. She couldn't imagine anything more thrilling than this. Because as much as Marianne craved marriage and a child, she never desired to be pregnant. So, for Marianne, adopting was not bittersweet, it was the sweetest thing she could imagine.

Over breakfast that morning, Marianne enjoyed the warmth of the sun as it streamed through her cream blinds. Her washed pine kitchen table was accented by cream ceramic tile. Everything was clean and bright and cheerful.

Angel's House

Before Marianne left, however, she took her shoes off and sat in the middle of her living room, yoga-style, and meditated. She quieted herself and listened to the God Spirit that she believed was in her heart and soul. Then she repeated several affirmations, "God is good. All that is good is streaming toward me. With God's guidance, I can achieve all my dreams."

Marianne was thankful that she had finally discovered God in her own way. When she was a young girl, she had told her mother, "Mommy, Tommy and Darryl called me blackie and ugly. Mommy, I'm not ugly, am I?"

"Of course not sugar. Come here. You are a beautiful little girl, and very smart too."

"Mommy, if I pray, will God make them be nice to me?"

"Pray if it makes you feel better, but I found that you can only count on yourself. You can do anything you want without any one else's help at all." Marianne's mother seemed to prove her point quite effortlessly. When her father had left them, Marianne's mother, who already had a bachelor's degree, went on to get her master's degree, and later claimed a high-paying job that kept the two of them quite happy. And even though her mother never remarried, she was a shining example of an independent, confident woman.

But over the years, Marianne realized that even if her mother didn't need Him, she did.

Recently, she had acknowledged that being so independent could be lonely. This form of prayer, meditation and affirmation, brought her peace.

She pulled on her cream blazer and headed downstairs to work. Today, she was dressed in cream, head to toe. The look made quite a statement.

About half-way to work Marianne knew something was wrong. Her BMW was acting up, making funny noises. This was the one thing Marianne hated. She felt that she could do anything a man could do, except lift very heavy objects and fix her car. Not that all men could fix a car, because she had met quite a few successful gentlemen that didn't know how to add windshield wiper fluid. But still, it aggravated her. And then it happened, kerplunk, weez and then nothing. There she was stopped half-way to work in the middle of the highway. Somehow she managed to get her car to roll to the shoulder. She tried to find her Triple A card to no avail. All she could find was a card with Joe's home number. She knew that she could have called information, but instead she called Joe.

"Hello?"

"Joe? This is Marianne. Are you busy."

"Not really, I'm going in late today."

"I need your help. I'm stranded on the highway. Can you believe it? Can you help me out?"

"Just tell me where you are and I'll be there."

Angel's House

Joe took down the directions and hurried to rescue Marianne. He looked under her hood and laughed. "Girl, do you take care of this car at all? Hand me that bag in the backseat of my car."

She waited while he fiddled around under her hood.

She smiled to herself as she glanced at the Toyota Camry he was driving. Nothing wrong with that, why didn't he just say he had a Toyota and leave that Benz story to the hundred other men who could use it?

"You're all set."

"Thanks Joe. What did you do?"

"Oh nothing. It's just a little secret us men folk keep to ourselves," he chuckled to himself.

Marianne was just happy because her car was fine. But now it would take everything
she had to go to work that day. It was one of those glorious days that everyone wants to skip work and go to the park.

"What's wrong now?" Joe asked.

"I don't even feel like going to work now. Half the morning's gone. I want to play."

Joe wondered what she had on her mind.

"Do you *have to* go to work today, Joe?"

"I don't *have to* do anything."

They spent the entire day together. First they went to the zoo. Next they took in a movie where they also ate hot dogs and nachos for lunch. Then they went to the park for a walk.

Before the day ended they made plans to go out Friday night.

Friday evening they met at a restaurant that was known to be the best steakhouse in town. There, they enjoyed each other's company as much as they enjoyed the food. Marianne had made a concerted effort not to ask Joe about his job or "his business". Somehow that made it easier. As long as she didn't know what he did, she didn't have anything to worry about. She knew this was foolish, but she couldn't help herself. Joe wondered too, why she avoided the issue. But he decided to go along with her, for the time being, because he enjoyed being with her so much.

After dinner, Joe followed her home to make sure she made it safely.

"I guess I'll see you soon," Marianne said.

"Yeah, I guess I'll see you soon," Joe replied.

Then Marianne said, "Would you like to come up for a drink or a cup of coffee?"

He said yes.

Angel's House

They walked into her dark apartment, and when she reached to turn on the light, he gently stopped her. He coaxed her to the sofa and for a moment just looked at her through the darkness. Then he leaned over and kissed her passionately. Quickly, he removed every single piece of clothing she wore, first her peach silk blouse then the peach skirt, the Givenchy pantyhose, the peach satin bra and matching panties. Before Marianne knew it, she was completely nude. The first thing he did was put his hands on her thighs and hips, caressing them. She flinched, thinking he thought she was hippy or flabby. But he was thinking, "Baby has back. Baby is fine."

Then he moaned, "Oh Marianne."

Somehow they ended up in her bedroom, atop her cool, cream-colored cotton sheets and it was there that they would have made love. But Marianne said, "Joe, do you have a condom?"

He started fumbling for his wallet.

"Oh Joe, it doesn't matter. Even if you did, I couldn't make love to you, not yet. We have so much to talk about. I don't even know what you do for a living. I know that I like you and that you're a nice guy. I'm sorry, I just can't, not yet."

"That's cool. Why don't I just hold you for awhile. I promise, no funny business. I just want to hold your body next to mine. We'll talk soon, but for now, let me just hold you."

Later in the night, Marianne woke to find Joe looking at her with his head propped up on one hand. He said, "Come here, girl." He cuddled with Marianne again, then he said, "I was thinking, why don't you adopt a little boy too."

Marianne turned around. "Now how am I going to take care of a boy and a girl by myself?"

Joe said, "Who said anything about you doing it by yourself?"

Chapter Eleven

Angela had gone back several times to meet with the Reverend C.J. Johnson to see if there was any way she could help his church.

It turned out that he and his church were already helping the community but that they always had more people to help than time or money. Mostly, he reached out to the youth, especially the young men and boys, encouraging them to stay in school.

Any help she could give them, he told her, would be appreciated.

Angela drafted and mailed letters to dozens of businessmen and civic leaders, requesting their help. She knew she had little chance of meeting with one person in particular, but she sent a letter to Christopher DeVreau anyway.

When his secretary called her several weeks later, she was very pleased.

Angela walked into Christopher DeVreau's office a little apprehensive because she had read so much about this man, how he had risen so quickly.

Her hair styled with large bouncy curls, she was dressed in a fitted black suit made of year-round wool and a lightweight red silk turtleneck. Even though spring had arrived, this was an especially cool day.

Walking into his office, she admired the mauve and grey carpeting, and simple, elegant decor.

"Hello Mrs. Castlestone. It's so nice to meet you."

Her hand reached toward his outstretched hand, her eyes met his and for just a moment, her heart fluttered.

Christopher was an intense, determined man. Handsome, with rich brown skin, a neat mustache, closely cropped brown hair, he was tall and muscular.

Angel's House

The kind of man that you just knew had played football in college, maybe even a couple years in the pros.

They shook hands and sat down.

"I'm very sorry about your husband. I read about his death a few months ago."

"You knew Baron?"

"No. But I read about him over the years and I really respected him."

"You know, actually, I remember Baron talking about you too. He kept saying you were poised to be the next president of your company, one of the first African-American presidents of a Fortune 500 company. He was very proud of you even though he didn't know you personally. I wish he had still been alive last month when you were promoted from senior vice president to president."

"Thank you for telling me that Mrs. Castlestone."

"Please, call me Angela."

"Okay, and you call me Christopher or Chris if you'd like."

"Sure."

"Well Angela, tell me how I can help you today."

"Christopher, since my husband passed away, I've

been searching for something more meaningful to do with my life. He left me quite a bit of money and since the Republican takeover I haven't been able to sleep very well at night."

Christopher laughed.

Even Angela had to smile at her words. "Anyway, I have an idea I think I want to pursue and I've been meeting with people to get ideas."

He saw a sadness pass over her face. "What were some of the ideas?"

"It seems that my husband's associates don't really understand what I'm doing. First of all, they have no fear of the Republicans and secondly they don't understand why I don't donate some money to medical scholarships and research. You know, because that's what they think Baron would have done. But I'm not Baron, I'm Angela. I want to do something of my own. I dedicated the last ten years to Baron's ideas and dreams. I miss him so much but..."

Christopher handed her a tissue when he saw her eyes fill with tears.

"But I need to make this break. Begin my own life. Do you understand what I'm saying? Am I making any sense at all?"

"Of course you are Angela. Please go on. I'm listening."

"Okay, thank you. I'll just get straight to the point. I'm considering donating money to a small church a few miles from here. It's called City Church. I have this feeling that this man can move mountains. He's already reaching out to the youth in that part of town and convincing them to stay in school and not commit crimes or join gangs. There aren't many men out there willing to reach out to these desperate young men and change their lives, convince them that there is a better way of life. I have no idea how much money he needs or even what resources are needed."

Christopher, smiling and intrigued, said, "Can I ask you why you wanted to talk to me?"

"Because I just figured a man like you would have some awesome ideas and feedback."

"I appreciate the compliment, but I hope you realize how awesome and smart you are too."

Before Angela could respond, Jessica, Christopher's secretary interrupted them.

"Mr. DeVreau your next meeting begins in two minutes."

"Thank you."

Christopher turned his attention back to Angela. "I'll call you in a week or so. I'll be out of town a few days, but we'll talk again real soon." He walked her to the door. "Angela, it looks like you think you can change the world."

Her feelings hurt, she said, "You sound so cynical Christopher, for a such a successful man." And then she slowly walked away.

He hadn't meant to sound condescending. He was trying to give her a compliment.

She hadn't meant to sound so emotional. Maybe he wasn't being condescending, she thought, as she slowly approached the elevator doors.

****

A week later, Angela sat alone in her kitchen eating a bagel slathered with cream cheese. Cally had the week off, so this was the first time she had been totally alone in some time.

She looked across the table at the chair Baron had always sat in and smiled sadly. In her imagination she could see Baron sitting there smiling at her and talking about an upcoming surgery. Sometimes she felt like he was still with her, trying to tell her something. She thought maybe he wanted to apologize because they never had children together. She hoped he wasn't lingering because his soul was guilt-ridden because that thought was too painful for her to bear.

She looked across the table again and he was still there looking at her like he wasn't sure how long this privilege would last.

"Baron," Angela began. She was embarrassed talking to a figment of her imagination but since she was

Angel's House

alone, she had nothing to lose.

"Baron, I'll be fine. Really. I'll have children one day, okay? You can go on now. Don't feel bad, this wasn't your fault."

In her mind though, he just shook his head. Because try as she might, she couldn't hide the pain in her heart, not from Baron.

"What do you want me to do? What do you want me to say? I just miss you so much. How could you do this to me? How could you leave me by myself?" Then the words came spilling out like too much water in too small a cup, "Sometimes I hate you!" Angela had lost control. Tears streamed down her face and sadness engulfed her soul.

"No Baron, I'm sorry, I didn't mean it. Baron?"

As she approached the chair his image began to fade, and by the time she reached the chair he was gone.

****

Later that afternoon, in contrast to Angela's dreary disposition, the sun shined brightly, the sky was a brilliant blue, adorned with puffy white cotton ball clouds here and there. It was warm outside, a perfectly glorious day.

Sitting on the deck just off her bedroom, Angela knew that if the weather hadn't been so kind, she might have lost her mind with sadness, loneliness and now guilt, for not being stronger. It was much easier to be the perfect wife than it was to be the perfect widow. She began to wonder how she could have prepared herself for this. She wondered if that was why so many couples were often cruel and distant. Maybe that was a safety mechanism for just in case.

She reached toward the phone to call anyone to keep her mind off Baron. Just before her hand could lift the cordless phone out of the base, it began ringing.

"Hello," Angela answered.

"Angela, it's me, Christopher, were you busy?"

"No, just relaxing out on my deck."

"I'm jealous. That sounds terrific. Listen, do you have plans for this evening? I thought we could go out to dinner and talk some more. Maybe Bradley's?"

"That sounds fine. What time?"

"I'll pick you up about six if that works for you."

"Great, I'll see you then."

Something to do. Thank God for something to do.

To offset her mood, Angela dressed in an orange linen skirt and a chiffon blouse with a peach, orange, coral and yellow floral pattern. She carried a tangerine-colored Chanel bag and wore matching leather, high-heeled pumps. The look was much more feminine and

Angel's House

frilly than her usual style but she hoped it would pick up her spirits.

It was fun getting dressed up to go out. And she hated spending so much time with her parents, Marianne and Caroline, because they had their own lives.

She walked gracefully down her staircase to answer the ringing doorbell.

"Christopher, it's so nice to see you again. Would you like to come in or shall we just go."

"I'm pretty hungry, why don't we just head to the restaurant?"

"Great! I am starving. My cook is on vacation this week and I am so spoiled."

"I know what you mean."

Christopher drove a brand new silver Lexus that fit him to a tea--elegant, smart, well-built, and easy on the eyes.

As they entered the posh restaurant, Bradley's, Angela remembered this was one of the last places she and Baron had gone. But she tried to force that memory as far in the back of her mind as she could.

"Mr. DeVreau, hello, how are you this evening?"

"Just fine."

Angela was annoyed, as many times as she and Baron had been here and this waiter was acting like he had never seen her before. What a joke.

"Is anything wrong Angela?"

"No, I'm fine. Thank you."

After browsing the menu, she asked, "Christopher, are you married?"

"No, actually I got divorced a few months ago, around the holidays."

"I'm sorry. Do you have children?"

"No."

Angela wanted to ask him why. She was very curious.

But Christopher went on, saving her the agony of asking. "My wife never wanted children. That was the source of a lot of our problems. One day she just told me that she wasn't going to ruin her figure for anyone. It took her years to finally tell me. She just kept stringing me along because we had such a good life together. You know, because of my career, prestige, money, clothes. It took me a long time. I just turned 40. You'd think someone like me would have caught on sooner."

"No. Don't say that. We all make mistakes."

Angel's House

"Well, I must be boring you to death. Let's talk about your plans for that church, City Church, right?" He wanted to get out of the hot seat. He hadn't planned on telling her so much but he trusted her and contrary to what people thought, men did hurt from divorce too, even successful men.

Her face lit up for the first time that evening as she began describing her plan.

"Okay, I already told you about the church and the minister, but there is so much more. Across the street from this church is an abandoned school. Busing really doomed a lot of these inner city schools. The whole idea helped ruin some of these neighborhoods too. It is so unfair for children to need to go miles away from their homes to get a decent education. I want to reopen this school with the church as a base. Quite a few of the church members are retired teachers."

She continued, "You know I can see this school with clean walls and swimming pools, the best equipment around. I can see happy children reading books that tell history the way it should be told. I see teachers who discover how each child needs to be taught and then taking action. I see morality, self-esteem, human sexuality and more being taught. I see the classics including Toni Morrison and Maya Angelou. I hear the joy of the children laughing and no hunger or fear when they are there. I can see a glimmering halo above the school protecting it against crime, violence, hatred and gangs. I see something that is possible, that should not be a dream, but reality for any child born on this earth."

"I can see it too. Go on, please tell me more." Christopher was mezmerized.

"The school would take in children from pre-school, age three, through twelfth grade. Economics should not come into play. Anyone who lives in that neighborhood should be able to attend. There are schools like that now but they are in the minority. None of the politicians are talking about education, they don't give a damn about poor children.

When the Republicans took over, I was stunned by their rhetoric. At first I couldn't figure out what troubled me so until recently. Christopher, I think we are under attack. African-Americans. I don't know what they're so scared of and to be honest I don't care. When they talk about how they want to get rid of welfare and affirmative action there is a frightening, Ku Klux Klan, we are tired of Black folks undertone. They want to strip away all the safeguards and go back to the way things used to be. I don't know about you, but I'm glad I'm living in this time period."

Christopher said, "To be honest with you I feel some of the same undertones but intellectually some of the ideas make sense. Welfare seems to have taken away the prides and wills of a lot of people."

"I agree with you."

"And affirmative action. Maybe it is outdated."

"I'll tell you this, I just knew that as the Republicans focussed on their determined list of 10 initiatives, that number 11, 12 or 13 would be: Get rid of Affirmative Action. That frightens me. So many people would be miles behind if it hadn't been for affirmative action. I just don't know what would happen if we got rid of it, if there weren't any laws."

But Christopher added, "That is an issue for Black people to consider because perhaps we will never know the possibilities if we aren't forced to live without preferential treatment. As long as Blacks get special treatment, they will be different."

"But Christopher I don't think it's about us being different. It's about the reality of the world. I guess I see affirmative action as an over protective mother making sure her children have a chance to play on a level playground. She walks her children to the playground and then forces everyone to play fair, or else. As the years pass, resentment builds because those Black children are taunted by others with, 'If it weren't for her, you wouldn't be here.' And then others who are their friends make them feel so comfortable that they begin to wonder if they ever needed her to protect them at all."

Angela added, "It seems that so many affluent and successful African-Americans are saying, 'It's time to put affirmative action to rest.' But I keep thinking, how easy that must be sitting comfortably in their ebony and ivory towers. How easy now that they have friends at the top: Black and White. The frightening thing to me is what if we lock her away in a closet and our younger brothers and sisters are beaten down by the bullies, the outright racists, and even kind-hearted liberals who are still ignorant and hire those who make them feel comfortable."

She ended, "One day we might need affirmative action again, but she may be too weak to be up to the fight."

"I never thought of it quite that way," Christopher said.

"Think about it Christopher. There was that book talking about the intelligence, or the lack there of, of Black people versus everyone else. Then there's this O.J. murder trial. Sometimes I wonder why people are so interested, it's almost like a public lynching. Then there are at least three Republican presidential candidates considering running on a platform that's against affirmative action. Then there's Ron Brown being attacked. Dr. Joycelyn Elders ousted just like that and the new Black man hoping to be appointed to the post fighting against fierce opposition from conservatives. And oh damn, the NAACP's financial problems, which are our own people's fault, but it all adds up to a bunch of mess. Instead of wading in the chaos, I want to find my own answers and do whatever I can."

"Well I have to tell you Angela, if anyone can do it, you can. We may disagree on a few things politically, but I have to tell you that I love your idea about the school. I want you to go for it and I'll support you anyway I can."

Angel's House

"You will?"

"Of course."

By this time their meal had arrived. He dined on filet mignon like Baron always did. And she enjoyed a shrimp and lobster bisque. They sat silently eating for a few minutes.

In a quiet voice, Christopher said, "I like being with you. It's hard being alone. To me anyway."

"It is hard. I may never remarry. I may never even have children," Angela added.

Christopher reached for her hand and held it gently. The wonderful thing for both of them was that in addition to the electricity they felt pulsating through their hands, they felt a deep affection and friendship, like they were meant to be each other's guardian angels.

****

Saturday, April 22, 1995

Dear Diary,

The emotions I feel are overwhelming. I feel the excitement of helping a community in need. I feel the joy of holding Christopher's hand. And still feel so much guilt for feeling happiness. I'm not sure if its just that it is simply too soon.

Alissa Whitehornne

Why does life have to be so difficult?

Angela

Chapter Twelve

The sun blazed brightly and arrogantly, because it was summertime, a time when the sun and its intense heat were welcomed.

The ladies luncheon was held at a fancy restaurant that specialized in barbecue. Outside on the patio, a small buffet of baby back ribs, grilled chicken, homemade potato salad, and strawberry shortcake was set up for Angela and her friends.

Angela and Marianne were seated and talking when Caroline arrived. Caroline's curly brown hair rested freely on her shoulders and her lips which were painted red, displayed a broad smile. She wore a brightly colored sarong-styled dress that was splashed with red, orange and yellow flowers. It tightly cinched her waist and showed off her round bosom and slender, shapely legs. And her high-heeled red leather pumps gave her the allusion of being several inches taller than 5 feet, 4 inches. She looked years younger and happier than she had in years.

"Look at you Caroline. You look gorgeous and incredibly happy. What is up with you?," Marianne asked.

The entire group turned to listen. Whatever she was doing, they wanted to do too.

"Well," Caroline began, "I think its mostly all the speaking I've been doing to these young women. It's really helping. I'm making a difference in their lives. Oh, and I left Marcus." She conveniently left out that she was also pregnant.

"What?," Marianne asked.

"It was time. But I don't want to talk about that. I'm happy and at peace. That's what matters."

Then Leslie asked, "Okay then what's up with you, Angela, and you too, Marianne? The three of you are glowing. What's the secret?"

Angela smiled. "There's no secret. We're just trying to make a difference in the world, the best way we can. It seems the more we try to help others the better our lives become." She left out her budding romance with Christopher. Her mind told her she should still be in mourning, but her heart told her otherwise.

Marianne said, "I'm adopting a little girl. I am so happy and excited. Like Angela and Caroline said, it started out as charity for others but we ended up gaining so much in return." She conveniently left out her relationship with Joe. It was too soon to share this secret with the whole group.

Leslie said, "It's all about giving? You guys like become little angels and God smiles down on you? And I have a feeling the three of you are keeping a few secrets to yourselves too. Well sign me up. I give back but I can give back even more too. At least now we know what you secretive ladies have been up to all these months."

Then she turned around to two ladies at her table. "Let's start our own group. What do you say? Shall we become angels too?" They shook their heads in agreement.

Leslie said, "As a matter of fact, I would be interested in joining or forming one of those groups that are fighting to protect affirmative action. To tell you the truth, I'm getting pretty annoyed with some of these Republicans."

"Leslie, I'm shocked. I thought you loved the Republicans," Angela said mockingly.

Leslie said, "Don't get me wrong. All Republicans aren't bad, most of them have a pretty good rap. But that small, increasingly vocal group, that wants to abolish affirmative action, is dangerous. Now I think I know how the freed slaves must have felt every time they made a step forward and someone decided to change a law that put them two steps back. If America is so wonderful why are they so frightened of laws and quotas? If you are fair, you shouldn't have a problem with affirmative action."

"But let's get real," she continued, "we all know of people who were told straight to there face that they were hired to meet a quota. And we know that many managers tell racist jokes and make racist comments to see how you will react in front of everyone else. America ain't ready to get rid of affirmative action. When I see those human resource people talking about how they strive for diversity but they don't want to be told what to do, I want to gag. What the hell is diversity anyway? That could mean I hire nice people and mean people, rich people and poor. Diversity doesn't mean a damn thing. Without laws to enforce a diverse workforce, Black folks will be in trouble. After this most recent recession, Black people were the only group of people who ended up with fewer jobs."

Then she looked at Angela and said, "All I know is that I'm going to do everything I can to save affirmative action. And if the Republicans do win this battle, I will

Angel's House

still do whatever I can to help young Black people continue to enter the workforce."

"You go girl!," Angela said, smiling. "You know Leslie, no one complains about having a police force to protect them against bad people. But to admit we need affirmative action's laws and quotas, is to admit that a lot of people in corporate america are racist, or at least ignorant. They just don't get it."

The last three ladies made plans themselves.

Leslie suggested that the ladies luncheon disband while each group pursued its goals.

"I'm going to miss meeting with all of you. We'll just have to get together around the holidays though, okay?," Angela said.

"It's a deal," Leslie said to Angela, then they shook hands. It was as if the three groups of women had signed their own Contract with America.

Chapter Thirteen

Marcus could not believe Caroline had left him. Actually, he was furious. After all he had done for her. He kept thinking about how ungrateful and unappreciative she was. When he first read her note he had gone into their family room to watch BET on their big screen TV.

When K-Ci from Jodeci came on the screen, he felt an immediate brotherhood. Marcus sang loudly with K-Ci, "If you think you're lonely now, wait until tonight girl. Yeeeeaaahhh. Wait until tonight girl."

Angel's House

That night before he went to bed, he mumbled to himself, "Yeah Caroline, you do what you got to do, but you're gonna miss me." He strutted across the room and got into the king-sized bed alone.

****

As the days passed though, Marcus starting missing Caroline. But his pride kept him from contacting her about reconciling. Instead, he threw himself even further into work. Several times he even considered picking up a young lady at one of the clubs. He knew he had the looks, the job and the car that would impress 99 percent of the young women who frequented the clubs. But he wasn't that type of guy. In all the years he had been with Caroline, he had never even come close to cheating on her. Sure, like most guys, he looked, and he enjoyed the admiration of women from afar. But that was it, because contrary to his behavior, he loved Caroline.

The only choice was to throw himself into his work.

Late one evening at the firm, a senior partner approached Marcus in his office.

"Working late again, Marcus?"

"I sure am."

"Marcus, how would you like to make partner here at our firm?"

"How would I like it? I would love it." Marcus' heart was beating fast and perspiration began to trickle down his temples.

"Well, the partnership is yours Marcus. You earned it. Congratulations."

"Thank you Jim. Thank you. You won't be sorry. Thank you."

"We'll talk more tomorrow. Have a good evening. You better get home to that pretty
wife of yours."

Marcus reached for the phone to call Caroline. The phone rang 10 times before he realized he was calling his house, where Caroline no longer lived. He didn't even know how to reach her, not that he would have called her. She left him. He didn't leave her. This was her loss.

Still, he called Angela and got Caroline's phone number. An answering machine picked up the call. He almost hung up because he didn't recognize this happy voice. Her cheerful voice spoke to him, "Hello, this is Caroline. I am so sorry I missed your call. Please leave your name and number and I will get back to you as soon as possible. Have a nice day."

"Uhm, Caroline. This is Marcus. I just wanted to see how you were doing. Well I just wanted you to know that I made partner at the firm. Not that you really care. But I just thought I'd let you know. I'll talk to you later."

Angel's House

After that, Marcus was feeling cocky. He thought she'd come running back now that he proved he was right, that he could make partner. He thought she wouldn't be able to resist being married to the partner of a prestigious law firm.

But after a week had passed, Marcus hadn't heard a word from Caroline. Maybe she didn't care about the partnership or the money he made. Maybe she really did want to spend more time with him like she told him the week before she left.

****

Caroline smiled for days after she got Marcus' message on her answering machine. She wondered if he missed her over the past months and this was the first sign that he did. But there was no way she was going to call him back. No way.

Caroline loved the home she was renting. It soothed and comforted her with warm, loving arms, unlike the home in which she and Marcus lived. That home was too big for the two of them. Even if they had had children, it would have been too big. She had always thought the house was gaudy, but Marcus loved it, like it proved to the world that he had made it. Two grey stone lions roared at the entrance of the home and the backyard was tiny and the new neighborhood hardly had any large trees at all, mostly puny ones that would take years to grow. Everyone in the neighborhood drove a Mercedes, a Lexus or a Jaguar. And she and Marcus were the only Black people in the entire neighborhood.

People thought being fair-skinned as she was had its privileges. And sometimes it did. But she was Black, loved being Black, and being thrown into an entirely White world was lonely. No matter how nice they were to her, it wasn't the same as talking to Angela and Marianne. How she longed for neighbors who looked like her. She heard about prestigious neighborhoods in other cities that were entirely Black and wished her city offered the same type of neighborhoods, but it didn't, not yet. Actually, she would have been happy with a neighborhood that had two or three Black families.

This new neighborhood, in which Caroline lived, gave her just what she needed. The neighbors were friendly and her Mercedes was the only one in sight. Children laughed loudly and played hard, birds sang in the large oak trees, and she felt welcome.

Caroline's baby continued to grow, and except for a few weeks of morning sickness, the pregnancy was going well. She calculated that she was about 14 weeks pregnant and figured it was time to go see the doctor. The funny thing was that even though she had gained a few pounds, she hadn't lost her figure yet. She was so happy she could wear that floral dress at the luncheon. She had to wear control top pantyhose, but it was worth keeping this secret to herself.

This sunny Saturday afternoon, it was hot and humid. The ceiling fans could only put a small dent in the heat. Caroline took another shower and slid into a pair of powder blue cutoff shorts and a peach halter top that revealed a still mostly flat stomach. Something told her to enjoy it. Something told her that very soon she would "pop" and her belly would protrude like most pregnant women's. She liked being slim, but if she did "pop" and continued to carry this baby, she knew she would be happier than she had ever been. And if she had to, she was prepared to raise her baby alone.

With no shoes on, her toes painted a peachy coral color, and her freshly washed hair, still wet and uncombed, she went into her kitchen and made a large pitcher of lemonade. She poured herself a large glass, filled with ice cubes, and went out onto the porch. She sat on the white porch swing and sipped the cold, tart sweetness of her lemonade. Caroline propped one leg up on the swing and let the other leg dangle as she closed her eyes and enjoyed a gentle breeze that pushed the swing.

The gentle warm breeze felt good in contrast to the stammering heat. Her eyes still closed, she soaked in as much of the breeze as she could. As she swung softly, she wondered what would happen to her and Marcus. She let her mind wander back in time, to a place where she was happy. She was happy now, alone. And she was happy years ago, with Marcus. What had gone wrong? Even though she mostly blamed Marcus because of his relentless ambitious, she knew in her heart that she had to shoulder some of the blame. She should have spoken up years ago when Marcus first went overboard. And why had she let his actions effect her so dramatically? Wasn't she ultimately responsible for own happiness?

She heard a car door slam but continued to daydream. From the cold glass in her hand, she felt cool droplets dripping onto her neck and shoulders. In her mind she could see Marcus holding her in his arms. Kissing her lips gently. She imagined his hands slowly untying her halter top and unzipping her...

"Caroline."

She opened her eyes to see Marcus standing above her, smiling. It took all the control she had not to turn beet red. If only he had known what she was thinking just moments ago.

Marcus stood above her clad in a pair of freshly pressed tan slacks, short-sleeved silk shirt and casual Italian loafers. As he peered above his dark sunglasses, he was thinking, "Damn! Caroline is fine." He didn't remember her ever looking so beautiful.

"Marcus, you surprised me. What are you doing here?"

"I just wanted to say hello."

"Did you miss me?," she asked.

"Of course."

"Good," she said, smiling mischievously.

Marcus sat down next to her and said nothing for about five minutes.

Angel's House

Finally, Marcus asked Caroline, "What went wrong?" He continued, "It seemed like we had it all. But I knew you weren't happy. To tell you the truth I wasn't happy either."

"You weren't Marcus? I thought all you needed was work. That's the main reason I left. I knew I couldn't compete with the firm."

"You never should have felt like you needed to compete with the firm in the first place. I don't know what to say or do. I don't even know where to begin."

"Neither do I. Marcus, would you like a glass of lemonade? There's more in the kitchen."

"No thanks. I'm playing golf with some guys this afternoon, so I better get going."

"Okay."

Marcus stood up and looked down at Caroline's pretty face. It was like looking at a ghost, at the innocent, sweet girl he loved so much and had fallen in love with so many years ago.

"You know I'll be back don't you? I'm coming back because I love you. I'm coming back because you are my sweetheart."

Caroline held in the tears until his back was turned.

He walked back to his sportscar slowly, like he wanted her to beg him to stay. He turned around to wave good-bye, just before getting in his car and speeding away.

****

When Caroline got the courage to see the doctor she was happy to hear good news. After scolding her for waiting so long to come see her, the doctor told her that this time it looked like everything would turn out fine. Caroline had snuck by the most dangerous first twelve weeks and was nearing her 16th week of pregnancy.

Over the coming weeks, Marcus called Caroline just about every other day, mostly about nothing, mostly just so that he could hear her voice. He felt guilty because she seemed so happy away from him. Had he been such a horrible person?

They were both frightened to talk about the deep issues for fear that a fight would erupt and forever cast a wedge between them.

Finally Caroline summoned the courage to invite Marcus over for dinner to talk about "things."

The dark, bluish purple sky displayed a million shining stars when Marcus arrived at Caroline's house late that evening.

She was dressed in a short-sleeved, lightweight denim sundress that flared out, starting at the waist, and went almost to her ankles. Again she wore no shoes. When Marcus noticed she wasn't wearing shoes again he was perplexed because Caroline always wore shoes or at least fancy slippers. She wasn't even the kind of woman who wore socks around the house. And now she wore no shoes as if it came perfectly natural for her to be barefoot. To him this was one of the biggest signs that she had changed. But then, way back in the recesses of his mind he remembered a 21 year-old Caroline studying in her dorm room without shoes, cut-off shorts, her hair wild.

"Hi Marcus. Come in."

"You look great Caroline."

"Thanks Marcus. You don't look too shabby yourself."

She led him into the kitchen. As he watched her from behind he thought she looked like she had put on a few pounds, not that she couldn't afford to gain a few pounds on her petite frame. It didn't matter to him though, and he knew there was no way he was going to ask her if she had gained weight and ruin the entire evening.

"Have a seat," she said.

Marcus sat down at the large wooden table and watched Caroline as she bopped around the kitchen putting finishing touches on their meal.

"Okay, we have shrimp salad, barbecue shrimp, steamed lobster and let's see, we have a tossed salad and some bread here. I guess I went a little seafood crazy, huh Marcus?"

"No baby, everything looks fine."

He called her baby tonight and a few weeks ago he called her his sweetheart. She thought she'd swoon. She had waited so long for him to show her this kind of affection again. They ate mostly in silence, then she got up to serve dessert, great big ol' ice cream sundaes, with chocolate and caramel dripping everywhere.

"Thanks for inviting me Caroline."

"Sure," she replied.

"I want you to know how sorry I am for the way I've treated you. I really am. I never meant to hurt you."

"You took me for granted."

"I know."

"You forgot about me."

"I know."

"You broke my heart."

"I know."

"But I should have been stronger. I shouldn't have allowed you to choose work over me. I should have given you an ultimatum a long time ago."

Angel's House

"An ultimatum?"

"Sure. But its hard Marcus. There are so few available, educated, successful men like you around that a lot of women put up with your crap, especially if you aren't hitting us or cheating on us. How dare we think we should be happy? But Marcus I am going to be happy. I've had a taste of happiness and peace. I could never go back to begging for your attention. I've changed."

"I know you have. I like it. You remind me of a young lady I used to know years ago."

Caroline smiled because she knew who that young lady was.

"Caroline, let me ask you something. Do you think the miscarriages played a big role in the demise of our relationship?"

"I think things were already going downhill, but well, after that, I needed you more than ever. I could never understand why you weren't there for me. Why didn't you comfort me Marcus?"

Marcus got up and walked into the dark living room in the front of the house. Finally, Caroline followed him into the living room.

"Marcus what's wrong? Are you mad at me for asking you that question?"

"No," Marcus replied in a distant, cold voice.

"Marcus, what's wrong, everything was going so well."

She knelt down at his chair and put her hands up to feel his face and felt a soft wetness. At first she thought he was perspiring, but it wasn't that hot tonight. Then she realized that he was sobbing.

"Oh Marcus."

She stood up and sat in his lap and hugged him. He held her tightly. Finally she got up though because she feared he'd touch her stomach.

She left him in the darkness and went out onto the porch. She listened to the crickets chirping in the freshly cut grass and rabbits rustling in the bushes. She looked up at the stars, searching for answers and wondering how long she could keep her secret.

The screen door creaked and Marcus approached her, his face now dry. He had regained composure. She felt sorry for him to have endured the pain she had felt.

He wrapped his arms around her and held her close. It felt good to comfort each other.

Just then though, in the middle of their embrace, an angel whispered to their unborn child. And being obedient, their son took his little foot and kicked as hard as he could.

"Whoah! What was that?," Marcus exclaimed, jumping back.

Angel's House

Then he looked at her standing there with her hands on her stomach like pregnant women do.

"Caroline? You're pregnant?"

She only nodded her head, ashamed for keeping her secret so long.

"When were you going to tell me?"

Then she got mad at him for questioning her. "When I got good and damn ready," she yelled. Then she started laughing. "Oh Marcus, I know it's a little boy."

He put his hands on her round belly and the baby kicked again. They sat down together on the porch swing watching the stars.

"Caroline, I'm so happy." Then fear crept into his voice. "Is everything okay? Are you okay? Is the baby okay?"

"Yes, yes, yes. Everything's fine."

At the same time they both leaned toward each other and kissed like they used to do. In the background they could here Black Girl singing on the radio, "Let's do it again. Ahh yeah!"

CHAPTER FOURTEEN

After Marianne and Joe's intimate evening, they both just happened to be very busy. She had several out-of-town technology seminars and when she returned, he told her he had business out-of-town as well.

Several weeks had passed when Joe called Marianne. "Hey girl, how ya' doing."

It felt good to hear his voice. "I'm doing great. How are you?"

Angel's House

"Fine. You know I missed you. I've had you on my mind. Boy have I had you on my mind."

Marianne was blushing. "Thank you. I missed you too."

"Are you busy tonight?"

"No."

"Then why don't you come over to my place tonight? We'll have dinner together and talk. How does that sound to you?"

"Perfect."

She took down his address quickly, said good-bye, and tried to get back to work. All that Friday afternoon, though, her mind wandered. Marianne felt at peace. She had already decided that she didn't care about Joe's occupation. She knew what she needed to know: that he was real, that he was kind, and that he liked her *a lot*. Over the past few weeks she had time to think it over and realized that he was the one for her no matter what he did. So Marianne was prepared to hear whatever Joe had to tell her, her sweet Joe.

On her way there, she was surprised to see that the closer she got to his apartment, the more exclusive the neighborhood became. When she finally arrived, she saw a large golden-colored Mercedes Benz sitting out front. It was one of those cars that you just had to stop and look at and wonder who owned it.

A doorman buzzed Joe, and then sent her on her way.

When Joe opened the door, she almost fainted. She was prepared for a small, average-looking apartment, maybe even something pretty nice, but this was unbelievable. Just from the door she could see cathedral ceilings, beautiful antiques, african art and windows everywhere.

"Joe. This...this is beautiful."

"Well come on in, so I can show you the rest."

Marianne was trying to regain her composure so he would not know how surprised she was. But it was too late, Joe was already smiling so hard he might as well have been laughing.

"You look surprised Marianne, what did you expect? Here let me take your purse."

"I don't know. I just don't know."

"Well let me take you on a brief tour."

Just then a young, slender White woman appeared out of no where. "Joe," she called. And Marianne thought she'd just die right then and there. What in the hell was going on?

"Yes Kathy?"

Angel's House

"What would you and your friend like for dinner? Would you prefer seafood or beef tonight? Any special requests?"

"Marianne, do you have a preference?"

"No, not tonight. Whatever you prefer."

"Kathy, I trust you. Prepare whatever you like. I'm sure we'll love it."

By now she was so shook up, she just wanted to sit down. "I'm feeling a little light-headed Joe. Can we sit down before the tour?"

"Of course. Why don't we sit in the living room and check out the skyline?"

On the way, Marianne saw a plaque on the hallway that said, "Joe Washington: Businessman of the Year."

Before they sat down, Kathy arrived with glasses of wine for both of them. Up close, Marianne realized that Kathy was not so young afterall, she looked more like a 50 year-old woman who hadn't led the easiest life. Being tall and slim with long blond hair, she had fooled Marianne. But what a relief.

"Kathy's great! I don't know what I would do without her. She comes by a few nights a week. She cooks extra meals too and freezes them. If it wasn't for her I'd be at Mickey D's all the time," Joe laughed.

But Marianne couldn't laugh she was still in too much shock.

"Marianne, are you okay?"

"Yes. No I'm not okay. Joe, this is not what I expected. I thought you were just Joe, my sweet Joe. I like you a lot and I was prepared to accept you for whatever you did. I just like you. Joe, I had no idea. But, who are you?"

"Who am I? I'm Joe Washington. The same guy I've been all these months. I told you I owned a business. I told you I had a Mercedes. It's out front. I told you how busy I was. Why are you so surprised?"

"But what about the Toyota that day?"

"It was a rental. I told you I would probably need a rental."

"Joe, I've been such a fool. I heard everything you said, but I have been lied to so many times that I stopped believing. You wouldn't believe the stories I've been told. I am so sorry. I owe you an apology."

"No you don't. You wanted me if I had nothing. You really wanted me for me. That's what matters. Just sit back and relax. We'll talk all night if necessary. Let's get everything out in the open. It's like I told you that first night. I don't have time to play games and I like you. Girl, I like you a lot."

****

Angel's House

It turned out that Joe owned several businesses. He owned a small soft drink company that currently sold to local retailers and he owned several detail shops throughout the city and the suburbs.

By the end of the evening Joe and Marianne were laughing and so engrossed in each other that they had completely lost track of time. By two o'clock in the morning they were both starting to nod off. "Stay the night," Joe invited.

"I don't know Joe."

"Listen, I've seen you completely nude and I held you for hours that way without losing control. Trust me."

He gave her one of his t-shirts to sleep in. They slept together in the same bed and nothing happened. It was fun, because they had a feeling that a no-touching, no-making love night wouldn't happen again.

The next morning, Marianne was awakened by the smell of bacon frying and fresh coffee brewing. In the kitchen, she found Joe singing softly. He seemed so happy.

"Good morning. What are you so happy about?," Marianne asked.

"I finally found the girl of my dreams. Wouldn't you be happy?"

Marianne just smiled. "I thought you didn't know how to cook?"

"I didn't say I didn't know how, I just said I didn't cook much. You just sit down and let me finish my cooking."

"Okay, okay," Marianne said. She sat in the modern kitchen with pale grey walls, black appliances and black lacquer dining set. She had never been so happy with any man.

"Now why are you smiling? What are you so happy about?"

"I found the guy of my dreams. Wouldn't you be happy?"

"Touche."

They quietly ate breakfast together when Joe began talking to Marianne looking very serious and a bit nervous.

"Marianne, I want to marry you. I know this is happening fast. But I'm decisive and I have excellent judgement. I want to marry you." Then he got down on one knee and knelt in front of Marianne, "Will you marry me?"

"Of course. Yes Joe, I'll marry you. I'm scared to death and I know things like this aren't supposed to happen. But who am I to question fate?"

Chapter fifteen

The depth of Angela and Christopher's friendship had grown over the months, from spring to summer, and now fall. Mostly they were friends, comforting each other, sheltering each other from the coldness of being alone. They held hands often and laughed frequently. Mostly they talked about her plans for the school, went out to dinner, and rented old videos. They loved watching movies like "Mahagony," "Sparkle," "Cabin in the Sky," and others.

Even though they both felt an intense chemistry, they were both frightened of a relationship and of ruining the friendship they had developed. He even listened to her with compassion this past summer when she told him that she thought she resented Baron for taking such good care of her. "Why did he have to take care of everything? Christopher, did he think I couldn't figure things out for myself once he was gone? He had plans for everything."

"Angela, that's just what men do, educated men of power and means. We take care of the women we love, all the people we love. We buy our parents homes, set up trust funds for our kids, and make sure our wives are taken care of. It's just how we show our love."

"Oh Christopher I know. I must sound so ridiculous."

"No you don't. He just took care of so much, you ended up with more time on your hands than you wanted. But you found great ways to fill the time. You've almost finished plans for the opening of the school. And you spend an awful lot of time with me," Christopher said, smiling.

"I know. I guess I've been pretty lucky."

"Angela, you do know too, that Baron did what he did so well because of you? You loved him so much that you were willing to sacrifice some of your needs in the shortrun. Everything would have worked out too, if he were still alive."

Angel's House

"Right. If he were still alive," Angela said.

"But Angela," Christopher said that summer evening, moving closer to her, "I think we could make each other very happy. Then he kissed her passionately. But she just froze. She was so frightened of what she felt happening to her body and her heart. So she just froze, cutting off all feelings.

"What's wrong?," he had asked her.

"I can't. It's too soon. I am so sorry. I just can't do this."

After that, Christopher backed off the romance, and held tight to their friendship.

But as fall arrived on the wings of burnt orange and toasty red leaves, Christopher was gathering the courage to approach Angela again about his affection. He was totally smitten with her. She was every bit as pretty as his first wife, but after that there were no other similarities. He thought Angela was one of the sweetest, kindest, most generous people he had ever met. He loved looking at her face, listening to her talk and watching her build a new future for herself. He just hoped she was including him in her plans. He secretly imagined what it would be like if they were married and had children, a boy and a girl of course. He knew that a life with Angela would be perfect.

While Christopher was warmed with hope by the burnished autumn leaves, Angela felt shivers. She feared the thought of pursuing a relationship with

Christopher. And as autumn ushered in the anniversary of Baron's death, guilt began to creep into her soul, telling her that she didn't deserve so much so soon. Deep in her heart she feared being hurt again. Here she was with all the money she needed, living in a mansion, and making plans for a new private school that would serve an impoverished neighborhood. How dare she think she could also have love too. What if she said yes to love and lost again? She wasn't sure she was strong enough to handle the pain.

****

On a cool fall evening in October, Angela and Christopher enjoyed a cozy dinner at a restaurant not far from where she lived. He decided to wait until they arrived at her house before bringing up how he felt about her.

As they approached Angela's front door, Christopher held her hand with anticipation. As she opened the door, he placed his hands around her waist. She turned around abruptly, "Chistopher, what are you doing?"

"Why don't we talk inside."

They stood in the middle of her massive foyer looking like two frightened deer. "Angela I know this summer you said you weren't ready for a relationship. But I was hoping you had changed your mind by now. I'm crazy about you."

"Christopher, you better go."

Angel's House

"What?"

"I've been thinking maybe we should stop seeing so much of each other."

Christopher stepped back. She might as well have slapped him in the face, kicked him in the shins.

She said, "You know I care about you. But I really need to focus on this school. The neighborhood needs it so bad. I've got so many plans, so much to do."

"Angela, you know I would never stop you from pursuing what was important to you. You know how supportive I am of you."

"I know Christopher. This is just a bad time. Thank you for a lovely evening. And thank you for your kindness." She stuck out her hand for him to shake. He took her hand in his but leaned forward to kiss her cheek.

"Angela, you know I'm not the kind of man to beg. You know where I stand."

Then he left, feeling like fall had disappeared with the harshest winter of all. Christopher had always gotten what he wanted. All his life he had won and now he was divorced from his heartless bitch of a wife and the woman he loved was rejecting him. People who read articles about him in magazines never would have imagined that their hero was suffering from a broken heart.

Alissa Whitehornne

****

Angela dug into her plans of the school like a mad woman. She made hundreds of phone calls, held nearly a dozen meetings at City Church, and studied mounds and mounds of research on what the school needed to be successful.

Every time a city official or a public school employee tried to tell her what she was doing was impossible she would just walk away because she knew she had to make this school a reality. She wanted to start a private/independent school with no ties to the public school system or the government. She wanted this school to belong to the residents of the neighborhood.

Finally everything fell into place because of her tireless efforts. It was now just time to wait. School would begin in a couple months, in January.

In the meantime, Christopher tried to get on with his life.

Late one night, his ex-wife showed up at his door dressed in a mink coat and high heels. She took off the coat to reveal a slinky black negligee.

"Christopher I miss you," Kara said with pouty lips.

Her gorgeous brown hair falling in her eyes, she moved closer to him. "Baby don't you miss me too?"

Angel's House

Since he was only human and very much a man, he wanted to carry her long, lean body upstairs and make love to her.

But instead, he asked, "Kara, why now? Why are you here?"

"Because I missed you. Come on, lets go upstairs and make love. Come on baby."

Then he looked into her eyes and he could see the manipulation. He knew she wanted something. But this time he wasn't going to fall for it.

"Kara," Christopher said.

"Yes darling," Kara said seductively.

"Put your coat back on and get the hell out of here. It's over. You know its over."

"You must be kidding."

"No I am not kidding," he said very deliberately.

"Well fine. I don't need you anyway. Many a man would be on top of this," she pulled a string to reveal her perfect breasts, "like white on rice."

She put on her coat and left, saying loudly, "You blew it Christopher. You blew it."

****

Angela sat out on her deck on a quiet Friday afternoon watching the golden and fire red leaves fall from the trees. She could hear leaves rustling from playful squirrels and eager rabbits too.

She sat there wondering what she should do next. She wanted to make sure she stayed busy. She decided that in order to keep her mind off Baron, and now Christopher too, she would begin making plans for a Christmas Eve party primarily for everyone involved with the development of the new school, but she would also invite her dearest friends.

Angela felt a warm breeze come out of nowhere and then hands upon her shoulders.

It was Baron. The first time, Angela thought she was imagining he was there, but now she wondered if he had become her guardian angel, watching over her and protecting her, from heaven no doubt.

He walked a few feet in front of her and leaned back against the deck as he admired the wooded, secluded surroundings. Then he turned to her, "Angela, I want you to be happy. This Christopher guy really cares about you. Don't throw it away because of me."

"But Baron, you're all I've ever known. I'm so scared. I thought we were going to grow old together. I chose you for my partner."

"Angela," Baron said, his eyes cast downward, "I'm dead. Claim the joy now, while you can. Please, please Angela, claim your joy now."

Angel's House

"But Baron, I keep praying to God, but he won't answer my prayers. I keep asking for peace, real deep down peace of mind and real happiness too."

"The Almighty, all-knowing God, Angela?"

"Of course."

"But Angela, did you ever ask yourself for peace and happiness?"

"What?"

"Angela, I thought you knew. God lives in you too. All the answers you seek, they are already there, but you have to listen. Trust yourself. Angela, I have to go now. Good-bye. But always remember that if you ever need me, I'll be here."

"Baron please, Baron please don't go," Angela pleaded.

"I'll be here when you need me, but Angela, you don't need me now. Maybe later, years from now, but for now, claim your joy. It's up to you and only you." And he was gone again. But this time he left her a gift only an angel could have left.

The warm breeze was gone and she could feel the coolness of the day again, but this time it felt refreshing.

She picked up the phone to call Christopher.

He answered the phone, "Hello."

"Hello Christopher, it's me, Angela," she said.

"Oh Angela, what a pleasant surprise to hear from you. How are things going?" he asked, as if he were talking to a business associate.

"Everything's fine," Angela replied. "How are things with you?"

"Oh business is fine. You know our stock recently went up."

"That sounds great," she said.

But she couldn't go on playing this game. "Christopher," she said, her voice softening and dripping with sweet honey, "I missed you so much. Do you still think we could be more than just friends?" She waited patiently for his reply.

"Could you repeat the question?"

"Christopher, I think you heard me."

"You already know the answer don't you?"

"No I don't. I know I hurt you."

After a few moments, he took a deep breath and said, "All is forgiven. Lets get this romance started," he said laughing.

"I can't wait," Angela said with total peace and confidence.

Angel's House

Christopher wasn't sure what had happened to change Angela's mind, he just knew that his prayers had been answered.

Chapter sixteen

Caroline and Marcus slowly moved toward the rebuilding of their relationship. They both agreed that they loved each other and that they wanted to raise their child together.

During the summer, Marcus had gone to the obstetrician with Caroline. At that appointment an ultrasound was performed. Their growing child seemed to be putting on a show for them. He danced and did little flips.

"Marcus, look, I think he's going to be a dancer."

"More like a gymnast," Marcus said, being macho. "Doctor, can you tell if its a boy or a girl?"

"Are you sure you both want to know?" she asked Caroline and Marcus.

"Yes, we do want to know," Caroline said. "We both hate surprises."

"Well, you know there is never a guarantee on this. Just looking at an ultrasound, I can only make an educated guess."

"Okay," they both said in unison.

"It looks like a little boy to me. If you look close right there, I think you'll see what I mean. Everything looks really good so far too. Just keep doing what you've been doing and I think you're going to have yourselves a healthy little boy."

Marcus and Caroline stared at the screen that displayed their little boy who appeared to be dancing and playing. They both had visions of what their new life would be like with a beautiful little baby son.

****

Now it was fall and Caroline and the baby were still healthy and growing. Caroline couldn't believe she was getting so big. Mostly, it was in her imagination though, because most people thought she looked great.

Caroline continued to live in the house for rent, while Marcus lived in the other house. They didn't want to rush things. Every time he asked her to come back she said she just couldn't move back in their house.

One fall evening, Caroline came home to her ringing phone. She picked it up just before the answering machine clicked on.

"Hello."

"Caroline, this is Alice. How have you been doing? Are you enjoying the house?"

"Oh yes Alice. It has been so wonderful staying here. I love it."

"Well dear, my sister passed away a couple days ago."

"Oh I am so sorry."

"Well the good lord took her away to a better place. She was in a lot of pain and she was starting to lose her faculties. Sometimes she couldn't even remember who I was."

Then it hit Caroline. Alice was coming back.

"Caroline, I'll be back in a few weeks. I hope that gives you enough time to make plans."

"Yes, that's fine. Again, I'm so sorry that your sister passed away."

Angel's House

"Thank you dear, I appreciate that. Now like I said, I'll be back in a few weeks, looks like around the 23rd of November, just before Thanksgiving. I'll see you then. I'll call you if anything changes."

"Thanks Alice. Good bye."

Caroline sat down in the living room on the sofa. She realized that all the time she thought she had was finally up. No more waffling. But she didn't want to move back into the other house. And it had nothing to do with Marcus and everything to do with that house.

A couple hours later, Marcus came knocking at her door unannounced.

"Marcus, what are you doing here? I didn't know you were coming by tonight."

"I had you on my mind. So I thought I'd stop by."

"It's nice to see you."

"You look upset Caroline. Is something wrong?"

"Alice, the lady who owns this house, called today to tell me that her sister passed away."

"Oh that's too bad."

"And that she'll be back November 23rd."

"Oh," Marcus paused and then asked her, "What are you going to do?"

"I'll tell you what I would like to do."

"Go on."

"Marcus, I want to be with you every night. But I don't want to live in that other house. I'm so happy here."

"You want to live in a house like this one?"

"Yes. It doesn't have to be just like this one, but similar."

"You want to sell our house?"

"Yes."

"You really hate that house don't you?"

"Yes, I do Marcus. I'm sorry if that upsets you at all, but we've been working on honesty here for the past months, so I'm being honest."

"I don't like it all that much either."

"Marcus! I thought you loved that house."

"Loved is the correct word. As in the past tense. Since I've been visiting you here, I can see why you love it here so much. There's a kind of warmth in this house and this neighborhood that is special."

"Marcus you don't know how relieved I am to hear you say that. I can't believe it. Another breakthrough.

Angel's House

We really are going to make it, aren't we?"

"Yes we are."

"But what are we going to do? We only have a little more than three weeks."

"Do you trust me?"

"Yes."

"I'll take care of everything. Don't worry about anything. Just sit back and relax darlin' and let ol' Marcus take care of you."

Caroline laughed at Marcus' phoney southern accent but she felt good knowing that she had nothing to worry about.

Marcus immediately put their house up for sale. Within one week they had two offers with only one catch: they wanted their furniture. When Marcus told Caroline, she was elated. "Please Marcus, tell them they can have the furniture. It won't fit in our new house anyway. Please Marcus, tell them yes."

Next Marcus went on an extensive search for the perfect house. Within a week, he narrowed it down to two houses.

The first house was located not far from the rented house. It was a little older than she hoped for, but it was charming and sweet.

The second house, though, was stunning, it offered everything the rented house offered and much, much more. The backyard was twice as large. And there were trees, trees and more trees, everywhere. The kitchen was large and stunning with skylights and an island in the middle. The porch was huge with a swing big enough for four people to fit onto.

"Marcus, how much is it?"

"It's $50,000 less than the house we're selling."

"Then this is it Marcus. I want this house."

"The builder just completed building it a few days ago. It's ours if we want it."

"I love it Marcus. I want it, but only if you do too. I mean it, only if you do too."

"I think it's perfect. It's the best of both worlds. If you want it, I'll put in a bid this afternoon."

Marcus and Caroline were doing the impossible. Selling a home, buying a new home, and moving in, all in just three weeks. But everything worked out just as they hoped.

****

A few days after they were settled in their new home, which was the Tuesday before Thanksgiving, Caroline and Marcus went to their first Lamaze class. A few minutes after class began, two young women came

Angel's House

into the room and sat down to listen to the instructor.

The pregnant woman looked over at Caroline and smiled.

Caroline thought she looked familiar but assumed she was just smiling because she was glad she wasn't the only Black person in the class.

Once the class was over, the young woman approached Caroline.

"You don't remember me, do you?"

"No I don't think so. Wait a minute, let me think."

"I'm from the Washington Projects. I met you in April."

"Oh yes. I thought about you for months. And I wanted to ask you your name but I couldn't find you."

"My name is LaShauna. It looks like we're both pregnant, huh?"

"Yes it does."

"But don't you worry about me. I'm gonna be fine. I'm finishin' school and then I'm going to college."

"That's great."

"I'm putting my baby up for adoption too."

Alissa Whitehornne

"Really?"

"Yes. After you spoke to us that day, I really started to think that I could do great things, like you said. Then I fount out that I was pregnant. I thought it was all over, you know like I was gonna be a statistic. But I kept thinkin' 'bout all the things you told us that day. I don't wanna give up my baby. But I know it's what I gotta do. All the girls in the hood, say I'm acting like a White girl, like I think I'm better than them. 'Cause ain't none of them give up their babies. But I know I'm doing the right thing. You think I'm doing the right thing?"

"Does that decision make you feel better about your future? Does it make you feel like you're going to be successful?"

"Yes m'am, and I ain't havin' no more babies till I finish school and have myself a job and a husband too. I wanna be like you."

"Thank you. Thank you so much for the compliment."

"No Mrs. Kelly, thank you. Thank you for talkin' to us that day. If you had come just a few weeks earlier, I probably wouldn't even be pregnant. But it's too late for that. I know I'm gon' make it. I know I can do great things."

"I know you can too. Good luck LaShauna. I'll see you next week."

Angel's House

"Okay. Bye."

"Who was that?" Marcus asked.

"Oh, just a little angel, uhm, I mean a young lady I met at one of my speeches. I'll tell you all about her later."

****

The next few weeks were wonderful for Caroline and Marcus. Their marriage grew stronger. And Thanksgiving was a time to be truly thankful.

Chapter seventeen

This was the happiest time ever for Marianne. She was making plans for a spring wedding, looking for a home to buy, her career was going well and she was getting closer and closer to adopting her little girl.

Finally, the day came that she had been waiting for all these months.

Angel's House

"Joe, the agency just called. They have a little girl they think I, we, would love to adopt. He asked me to come by later this afternoon."

Marianne was so nervous she was shaking.

"Calm down Marianne. Everything's going to be fine. This is what you wanted."

"I know. I'm just so excited and nervous and scared. I've waited so long."

She and Joe went together to meet with Mr. Jackson.

He shook both of their hands.

"Have a seat. Would either of you like something to drink, a soda, coffee?"

"No thank you," she said.

"I know you've waited a long time and we think you will be pleased with who we found for you."

He handed a large manilla folder to Marianne.

She opened it to find photos of the girl and a description of her past, medical history and education. Marianne handed the folder to Joe and started crying. First softly, then she couldn't stop.

Joe knew she would be happy and Mr. Jackson had seen many overjoyed new parents but never had he seen someone so emotional.

Joe finally asked her, "Is something wrong Marianne? The little girl looks adorable. Are you alright?"

"Yes Joe, I'm fine. I apologize Mr. Jackson. I'm fine. It's just that that little girl is the same little girl I took into foster care this past spring. I had no idea I'd ever even see her again. There was no warning."

When Mr. Jackson realized what happened he was very apologetic. "Oh Ms. Jones I am so sorry. Our wires must have gotten crossed somehow. I thought you knew. I am so sorry."

"No don't be sorry. I just didn't know. I have never been so happy in all my life. Thank you so much."

It turned out that the little girl's mother had gotten back on crack again and she started neglecting her again, leaving her alone for days. Finally, someone called the authorities and this time she lost all rights to the girl. It appeared that she was not physically abused but she had been severely neglected.

"You are very welcome. We'll be bringing her to your house Christmas Eve if that's okay with you."

"It will be the very best Christmas present I ever got," Marianne said, smiling at Joe.

On the way home, Joe asked Marianne, if there was anything else she needed to tell him about the little girl. Her uncontrollable crying frightened him because so far as he knew that was uncharacteristic of Marianne.

Angel's House

"There is one thing I never told you. After I lost her, I dreamed about her every night. I never forgot about her, not one single day. I couldn't talk about it because I thought there was nothing I could do about it. But after we get settled with her and get married, I want to do something that will help children, maybe help develop parenting classes or work on some committee that monitors the foster care system. I can't bear the thought of hundreds of little girls and boys like her suffering because they have worthless parents. I can't bear the thought of any more children dying in fires deliberately set by their parents. If I hear about one more boyfriend killing his girlfriend's baby or toddler, I think I am going to scream. This madness has to stop."

"I think that's a good idea because once the Republicans finish there won't be any programs available to help these people. Things will get worse for a while anyway. I guess its up to us take up the slack."

CHAPTER EIGHTEEN

On the morning of Christmas Eve, Angela awoke to the sound of Christmas music. Cally had arrived early and had already started playing the holiday CDs. Angela threw on a pair of Ralph Lauren jeans, a jean shirt, and a pair of tennis shoes. She'd spend more time later, getting dressed. For now she needed to finalize plans for this evening's party.

The cleaning people, who she and Cally would supervise, would be arriving any minute. Later that afternoon, she and Cally would put up the final decorations.

Angela took time out, however, to call Caroline to see how she was doing.

"Angela, I just got back from the doctor. She said it could still be weeks before I deliver. But I feel awful, my legs ache, my back hurts, I can't sleep and I can't stop cleaning the house. I keep rearranging and organizing everything. I'm going nuts."

"I heard things get pretty weird near the end Caroline. I'll pray for you. I hope you'll start feeling better."

"Thanks Angela. Because I am getting no sympathy from Marcus. All the guys at the office told him that their wives cleaned like mad right before they went into labor so he is too excited. But Angela, the baby's not officially due for another three...oh boy that hurt, another Braxton Hicks I guess, I hate these false contractions. Anyway Angela, I was saying the baby's not due for three weeks."

"Try not to worry Caroline. Try to relax, okay?"

"I will, and we'll try our best to make it to your party tonight. But I can't make any promises. I really feel...oh God...there's another one. I better go Angela. I better lie down."

Angela whispered a prayer for Caroline and hoped she would be fine. Mostly, she was happy that their friendship had mended itself over the past year. She was very happy because she had missed the old Caroline.

Then she called Marianne.

"Angela it's so good to hear from you. Girl I am so busy. Our little girl will be here any minute. Oh, there's someone at the door now. I'll call you back, okay? I love you. Thanks for calling. Bye."

Marianne sounded very happy. Angela whispered a prayer for her too, hoping that she would have a joyous Christmas with her fiancee and her new daughter.

Then Angela continued putting together the finishing touches for her Christmas Eve party. For the party, Angela let Cally hire a catering company to help out. Cally seemed so excited, but Angela thought she saw a look of envy in her eyes when she talked about the Black lady who owned the company.

"Cally have you ever considered starting a catering business?"

"Me? Are you kidding Ms. Castlestone and leave you? No, no."

"You've never considered it?"

"Well maybe when I was younger. I used to dream about owning my own business. But that was then."

Angela could see straight through Cally. This Christmas Cally would get a bonus that would be big enough for her to start her own business if she chose too. It was up to her.

Angel's House

Angela didn't want to stand in the way of Cally's dreams, she wanted to help her achieve them, if she could.

Angela went out to run a few last minute errands.

****

All the plans had been made and the invitations sent for Angela's Christmas Eve party. One thing had continued to nag at her though. Her house was so large and could be perceived as pretentious. She didn't want some of the people to feel intimidated or to call her Mrs. Castlestone (instead of Angela). So, she had found a friend of a friend who knew someone who painted signs.

The painter, James Smith, showed up this afternoon with his ladder, paints and instructions and went to work. He placed a beautifully painted sign just above her door. It was almost quaint, like a sign you'd expect to see in front of a little house in the country. He only made one mistake when he read the instructions.

When Angela arrived home she was happy to see that the painter had come and gone. The pretty little sign read, "Angel's House," not Angela's House as it should have. Not knowing he had made a mistake, Mr. Smith had even taken the liberty of painting tiny little angels at both ends of the sign. But, it was too late to change it and he had done a good job.

Angela went upstairs to bathe and get dressed. Following a relaxing bubble bath, she dressed in a silky black pant suit and high-heeled black velvet pumps. She pulled her hair atop her head and let strands fall softly into her face and onto her neck. She painted her lips a vibrant red and put on diamond earrings and a tennis bracelet. Today, she took off her wedding band. She was trying to move forward and put the past behind her.

About 5 o'clock Marianne called to tell her that she wouldn't make it to the party because her little girl had a cold.

"I understand. I hope she feels better soon."

"Oh she'll be fine. She's in safe hands now."

Then her phone rang again. This time it was Marcus.

"Angela, we just had a little baby, a little boy," Marcus' excited voiced boomed through the phone. "He's healthy and Caroline's fine. She said she'd call you later, she's nursing the baby now. Oh yeah, I guess you know we won't be able to make the party tonight," he said laughing. "Well, I have to go Angela. I have a lot more calls to make."

He was so excited, Angela hadn't had the chance to ask him any questions. She sat in her living room for a moment, thinking about how well her friends' lives were turning out when the doorbell rang.

Angel's House

It was Christopher looking especially handsome and dapper, with a fresh hair cut, and dressed in black slacks and sweater, a grey and black plaid blazer and black dress shoes by Bruno Magli. He arrived about 5:30 pm, a bit early for Angela's Christmas Eve party.

"Welcome," Angela smiled, "to Angel's House."

She and Christopher laughed. As she closed the door behind him, he placed his arms around her tiny waist and kissed her softly. His hands gently caressed her body. He felt her melting in his arms and he could feel the joy and excitement rising within him.

As he stepped back, he said, "Angela, I've fallen so deeply in love with you."

She replied, "I'm falling too."

She took his hand and walked him over to a large leather chair in her living room.

She sat down in the chair and he sat down on its cushiony arm. The fireplace was filled with bright flickers that seemed to dance and the large tree was decorated with golden bulbs, golden bows and pretty little angels.

In the background, Nat King Cole sang "The Christmas Song." Angela and Christopher sang along softly, "Chestnuts roasting on an open fire, jack frost nipping..."

"Angela," Christopher looked down at her and said, "Are you still keeping up with the Republicans? Have you heard about the latest debate?"

"No I haven't. I've kind of tuned them out for a while, so I could focus on what I could do. They upset me so."

Then he asked, " '95 turned out so well, what do you think '96 has in store?"

Angela just smiled because she saw a little angel on the tree come to life for a moment, smile and wink.

What Angela didn't know was that Christopher saw her too.

****

Suddenly, Christopher sprang to his feet. "Angela, I'll be right back. I left your gift in the car." He returned with a large box wrapped in gold foil and topped with a gorgeous green and gold bow. "Merry Christmas Angela."

This time Christopher sat in the chair and Angela sat on the floor like an excited kid who couldn't wait to open an early Christmas present.

Inside the box was a smaller box and inside that one an even smaller one. Angela kept looking up at Christopher smiling and laughing. To her the scene was so corny and funny.

Angel's House

Finally, she got to a small jewelry box.

Maybe this wasn't so corny after all.

Inside she found a two-and-a-half carat diamond ring surrounded by ice blue sapphires.

"Oh my God!," she thought.

"Angela, will you marry me?," he asked.

She rose to her feet and turning away from him, she walked toward the mantel and covered her face with her hands.

Christopher became embarrased for a moment. Was she laughing at him?

She turned around finally, smiling and crying all at the same time. "Yes, of course I'll marry you. I love you so much."

Then the angels sang as loud as they could without being heard,

"Hallelujah,
Hallelujah,
Hallelu-jah-yea!"

****

Alissa Whitehornne

December 25, 1995

    This is the best Christmas of my life. I finally have a beautiful baby boy, my marriage is stronger than ever, and I am truly happy. This past year has been remarkable. I have been truly blessed. I better go now. The baby's crying. What a beautiful sound. (Smile)

Caroline

****

December 25, 1995

    Everything has turned out so magnificently. A year ago, who would have thought that I would end up a year later with a daughter and a fiancee? You just never know what will happen in this life. I only have one thing to say: "Thank you God."

Marianne

****

December 25, 1995

Dear Diary,

I finally found peace. I guess Baron was right all along.

Angel's House

The peace and the happiness were there if I was only willing to trust myself and listen to God's voice. Christopher has been a godsend and everything that has happened has made me stronger. I just want Baron to know that no matter what, I will always love him too, and a special place will always be reserved in my heart just for him.

Thank God for Baron and all the other angels who watch over us.

Angela

The End